THE WIDOW AND THE CONMEN

"What brings you here this morning?" Dorna asked.

It took a moment for Ezak to tear his gaze from the shelves of magical items and reply, a delay long enough that Kel almost said something himself. He was deterred, though, by not knowing what to say—why *had* they come?

"Oh, we just wanted to offer our condolences, and to ask once more whether there is a anything we can do to aid you in your time of sorrow."

"Ah," Dorna said. "As a matter of fact, I've been thinking about your offer."

Ezak swallowed. "Oh?"

"I don't think I need any advice; I can make up my own mind on most matters. If you really just want to be helpful, though—well, as you can see, my husband had a good many talismans. With Nabal gone, I don't think I want to stay here in the village. I thought I might go to Ethshar of the Sands and buy myself a little tea shop there to keep myself busy. I'm very fond of tea. I can sell some of Nabal's magic to other sorcerers there to pay for it—there really isn't anyone around here who could buy them, but in Ethshar there are *dozens* of sorcerers. The thing is, all these talismans are a lot to move, and a woman traveling alone with valuables is at risk. If you really want to be helpful, perhaps you could assist me in transporting them, and accompany me to the city?" She smiled, and Kel reconsidered his opinion of her appearance—when she smiled, she was much prettier than he had realized.

"We'd be *delighted* to give you a hand," Ezak said, smiling back at her.

LEGENDS OF ETHSHAR

THE SORCERER'S WIDOW

LAWRENCE WATT-EVANS

WILDSIDE PRESS

Published by Wildside Press, LLC
www.wildsidebooks.com

ONE

Kel shaded his eyes against the bright afternoon sun and gazed at the little cluster of buildings ahead. "Is that it?" he asked.

"I suppose so," Ezak replied, walking steadily up the path. "We followed the directions."

"It's tiny," Kel said, hurrying to catch up. "I see..." He paused and counted silently, jabbing his forefinger at the air, then said, "I see just six houses."

"Four," Ezak corrected him. "One's an inn and one's a blacksmith's forge."

"Four," Kel said, musing. "Four? Just four houses?"

"Just four. But there are at least thirty or forty families on the farms around it."

Kel glanced at the surrounding fields, and the scattered houses of the families that tended them, then turned his attention back to the village ahead—if so small a gathering could even be called a village. "This sorcerer lived in one of the four?" he asked.

"That's what Uncle Vezalis said."

"Who lives in the other three?"

Ezak turned up an empty palm. "Who knows? Some of the farmers, I suppose." He gestured at the fields. "Somebody must be growing those crops, after all."

"Oh." Kel once again looked around at the vast expanses of knee-high green stalks. "Is that wheat?"

"*I* don't know," Ezak said. "Do I look like a farmer to you? I haven't been outside the city walls any more than you have. It could be wheat or beans or pumpkins, for all I know."

Kel frowned. "I don't think it's pumpkins."

"Neither do I. Now, smile and wave—there's someone looking at us." He suited his own actions to his words, and Kel, seeing the two women standing in the cleared area among the six buildings, waved vigorously.

"Do you think one of them is the sorcerer's widow?" Kel asked, lowering his hand.

"Probably," Ezak said through his forced smile.

The two women were definitely watching the two young men approach; one of them waved back, a single quick gesture. The women were of very different heights but appeared to be similar in age—past the flower of youth, but not yet gray and wrinkled.

A moment later the two men marched onto the little patch of bare earth that served as the village square and the village's only street, then stopped and stood facing the two women. Kel realized the shorter woman was no taller than he was himself.

Ezak slid his pack from his shoulder and said, "*Hai!* We're looking for the home of Nabal the Sorcerer."

The two women glanced at each other; then the taller, darker one said, "I'm afraid Nabal's dead."

"Yes, we had heard," Ezak said. "We came to pay our respects, and to help build the pyre."

"You're too late for *that*," the dark woman said. "We spread his ashes on the fields a sixnight ago."

"Ah, what a shame!" Ezak slumped visibly. "He was a good man."

The shorter woman spoke for the first time. "You knew Nabal?"

"We were apprenticed to the same master," Ezak said proudly.

The two women looked at each other. "You must have come well after him," the tall woman said.

"He made journeyman just as I turned twelve," Ezak said, spreading empty hands. "He left in Rains and I started in Greengrowth of the same year, but I used to hang around and pester him when I was little."

"You don't look that old," the tall woman said.

Kel glanced worriedly at Ezak. The story seemed to be getting out of control—how old *was* this Nabal? Ezak just smiled. "Well, thank you! I've been told I look younger than I am."

Kel looked at the women, unsure whether they were convinced. He could not read their expressions.

"What did you say your name was?" the shorter woman asked.

"Ezak of Ethshar," Ezak said. "Ezak the Sorcerer."

"Who's he?" the taller woman asked, pointing a thumb at Kel.

"Oh, that's Kelder. He's a friend of mine—it's a long journey to make alone."

"Kelder. Just Kelder?"

"We call him Kel," Ezak offered.

Before anyone asked, Kel volunteered, "I can talk. I just don't, much."

"To whom do we have the honor of speaking?" Ezak asked quickly.

The taller woman said, "Irien the Innkeeper." She gestured toward the nearest building. "I have a room if you need one. This is Dorna. Nabal's widow."

"Ah!" Ezak turned to the shorter woman and bowed deeply. "My sympathies on your loss."

"I'm sorry, too," Kel murmured.

"Thank you," Dorna said, with a bob of her head.

"I'm sorry we missed the funeral," Ezak said. "I really did want to see his soul on its way. Is there anything we can do for you, then, to make up for our tardiness?"

"No, I don't think—"

"Could you perhaps use our assistance with his talismans?"

"No, I—"

"I mean, you've lived out here all your life, while we're from Ethshar—perhaps we could give you some advice on how to get the most money for whatever trinkets he might have had."

"Honestly, I'm fine," Dorna said. "I haven't decided yet what to do with his things. There's no hurry."

"Oh, of course, I'm sorry. I didn't mean to rush you," Ezak said. "You take your time, all you want, and you can find us when you've decided. Meanwhile, dear Irien, you said you have a room? Even if we've missed the funeral, we've no need to rush off—this is such lovely country around here! Such fresh air!" He thumped both fists on his chest as he drew a deep breath.

Kel watched this without comment, and did not imitate his friend; he thought the air out here smelled funny.

"I have a room, if you have money," Irien said.

"Of course." Ezak jingled the purse on his belt. Kel knew half the "coins" in it were just metal scraps Ezak had picked off a tinker's floor, but the innkeeper didn't.

"This way," she said, gesturing.

The two men picked up their packs and followed her into the inn.

Ten minutes later they were alone in a stuffy gable room overlooking the village square, Irien having promised to bring them up a pitcher of wash water. Ezak opened the casement, then settled onto the surprisingly-generous bed.

"I don't think the widow recognized your name," Kel said, as he looked out the open window at the brown dirt square, the white and brown houses, and the endless green fields beyond.

"Of course not," Ezak said. "I never met this Nabal. My uncle knew him because they did some trading, that's all."

Kel had suspected that, and he had indeed partly meant that Nabal had apparently never mentioned Ezak, but he had also been relieved that Uncle Vezalis hadn't, either. "You *said* you knew the sorcerer."

"I lied. I want her to trust us. It'll make it easier to get all his magical things away from her."

Kel had feared that it was all lies. He knew that Ezak had never been apprenticed to a sorcerer. He had hoped there might be some trace of truth in the story, but apparently there was not. "It's funny that you lie to her to make her trust you."

"Well, life can be strange. It seems to work that way."

A bird sang outside the window. Kel spotted it on a nearby cornice, and did not recognize it as any sort he had ever seen before. Most of the birds he was familiar with were sea birds, and would not be found this far inland. "Thank you for not telling her my full name," he said.

"You're welcome. What should I tell her if she asks, though? There could be half a dozen people named Kelder around here; she may want an appellation."

"Anything. Just not Kelder the Blabbermouth."

"Or Kelder the Bastard, either. We'll just say Kelder of Ethshar, then?"

"That's good." He watched as the bird flew away, then asked, "Are you going to *steal* the sorcerer's things?"

"I'm hoping I can convince her to give them to me, or maybe sell them to me cheap, but I'll steal them if I can't get them any other way."

"I don't want another flogging."

"I don't want you to get one. I don't intend to get caught this time."

"You didn't intend to get caught last time."

"Well, I *didn't* get caught, did I?"

"But *I* did."

"Yes, and thank you again for not telling anyone it was my idea."

Kel turned up a palm. "It wouldn't have done any good. They were going to flog me anyway. I didn't want to be a blabbermouth."

"Thank you, all the same. So what did you think of the sorcerer's widow?"

Kel considered that for a long moment before replying, "She isn't very pretty."

"She isn't ugly, either, and I suppose old Nabal didn't have much to choose from out here in the middle of nowhere. She probably looked better when she was younger."

"Maybe he didn't worry about looks."

Ezak grimaced. "He was a sorcerer—the only magician in the village, maybe the only one in the entire region. He must have had his pick of all the girls here, so she must have been the best available. Which doesn't say much for the local women, does it?"

"Maybe she's smart, instead of pretty."

Ezak snorted. "If she was smart, would she be living out *here*? This Nabal couldn't have been all that bright, either, even if he was a sorcerer."

"Then how did he get to *be* a sorcerer?"

Ezak turned up an empty palm, then fell back onto the bed, where he lay staring up at the carved beams of the ceiling. "He served an apprenticeship, like anyone else. You don't need to be a genius to get through six years of running a master's errands, or nine, or whatever it is for sorcerers. All you need to call yourself a sorcerer is your master's say-so and a talisman or two." He glanced toward the window. "But according to my uncle, this one had a lot more than one or two. Uncle Vezalis said this fellow had *dozens* of talismans he'd picked up somewhere. Those are what we're after. This Nabal claimed he'd found a cache of stuff some Northerners hid during the Great War, but he was probably just trying to make it sound better than it was. I'd guess he inherited them when his master died." He flung himself back on the bed.

"His master died?"

"I assume so. I don't really know."

"You said you served under the same master—shouldn't you *know* whether he died?"

Ezak raised his head to glare at his friend. "Blood and death, Kel, I don't even know his *name*! If anyone asks us about him, we're just going to have to be vague, and change the subject as quickly as we can."

Kel considered that for a long moment, then said, "I don't think coming here was a good idea, Ezak."

"What are you talking about? Of course it's a good idea! A poor country widow with a houseful of sorcery and no children—we'll be rich!"

"You're sure she has no children?"

"Uncle Vezalis said the sorcerer was childless."

Kel considered this for a moment, imagining possibilities Uncle Vezalis might have missed—stepchildren, estranged children, siblings, cousins, in-laws, and so on—that could complicate matters. Then he said, "I don't like your story, Ezak. I don't think you know enough to fool her."

Ezak sat up to stare at his companion more easily. "I most certainly do," he said. "I don't need to know the master's name; I can just call him 'Master.' And I don't need to know whether he really died; if I get it wrong I can just say I was misinformed. My story is that I served my apprenticeship and then headed for Ethshar—I wouldn't be up to date on the local news."

"Do you know *where* Nabal served his apprenticeship?"

Ezak waved vaguely. "Some other village near here."

Kel did not reply in words, but the expression on his face made it clear he was not impressed with this answer.

"Kel, it'll be *fine*," Ezak said. "She's just a country bumpkin. It'll be as easy as finding sand on a beach."

"I don't want another flogging," Kel repeated.

"Look, even if it doesn't work, we won't be flogged! You think they even have a magistrate around here? Look at this place! If anything goes wrong, all we have to do is leave; no one's going to bother coming after us. They won't have any way to know which way we've gone!"

"They could use magic to find us," Kel said.

"No, they can't," Ezak said, grinning. "The only magician this village ever had was Nabal the Sorcerer, and he's dead."

"I thought…" Kel began, but then he stopped. It was obvious even to him that a village this small couldn't support more than one magician. "I still don't like it," he said.

"You don't need to like it, you just need to do what I tell you to, and we'll both be rich. Now, let me think just what…"

He never said what he wanted to think about; a knock on the door interrupted him, and Kel admitted Irien with a pitcher and basin, and a few small towels. As she set the basin on the bedside table Ezak got to his feet.

"Thank you, my dear," Ezak said, bowing deeply. Kel said nothing, but just watched, and nodded when the innkeeper looked his way.

"Supper's an hour after sunset," she said.

Kel glanced out the window again, and saw that the sun was brushing the treetops on the western horizon.

"Thank you," Ezak repeated. "We'll be down soon."

Irien left them, and Ezak closed the door behind her. "It was a long walk from Ethshar," he said. "I'm going to take a nap before supper. Wake me, will you?"

"All right," Kel said, as Ezak climbed back onto the bed.

That was the last thing Kel said for the next hour, as he sat by the window, staring out at the countryside as the sunlight gradually faded from the sky, and darkness crept over the fields and houses. Ezak was quickly asleep; Kel ignored his gentle snoring. For one thing, the snoring was a sign that the bed was soft and comfortable, which gave Kel something to look forward to. He knew that Ezak never snored when sleeping on hard ground.

He awoke his friend with a single soft word when he judged the time was right, and the two of them headed downstairs.

At supper Ezak asked Irien whether Dorna might be joining them, and was clearly disappointed when Irien said no. The sorcerer's widow kept early hours, the innkeeper said, or at any rate did not often venture outside after dark. If the two strangers were determined to see her, Irien said, they could call on her in the morning.

Ezak assured her that they would do just that, and thanked her for the suggestion. He was obviously eager to see more of Dorna, but Kel did not see what the hurry was about. This delay would give Ezak more time to plan, and Kel thought he could use it.

He did not say anything at the table, of course; in fact, his dinnertime conversation was limited to asking for plates to be passed, or thanking Irien for the various foods. Back in the upstairs room afterward, though, he asked why Ezak was rushing so.

"Two reasons," Ezak said. "Firstly, the longer she has to think about it, the more likely she'll settle on some way of disposing of her husband's magic where we can't get at it. And secondly, we just barely have enough money left to pay the bill for two nights here; if we're still here for a third, everything gets more complicated."

"Oh," Kel said. "So you want to steal the sorcery and get out quickly?"

"Exactly."

Kel nodded. That made sense to him. There was only one thing more to say.

"Good night," he told Ezak, as he climbed into bed.

TWO

The dead sorcerer's house was the largest of the four that surrounded the square, though still not exactly a mansion; Kel judged it to be roughly the same size as the inn. A line of black ash marked the red-painted front door, indicating that the occupants of the house were in mourning. The country around them smelled of moist earth just now, a scent that reminded Kel pleasantly of cellars, and a warm spring breeze stirred the air as he waited for Ezak to knock.

Ezak rapped gently, careful to keep his knuckles well clear of the ash.

"Who is it?" Dorna's voice called.

"Ezak of Ethshar."

"Just a moment."

Kel wished that Ezak had mentioned that he was there, too; he didn't want to startle anyone. He didn't want to call out himself, though, so he waited silently.

When Dorna opened the door she didn't seem surprised to see him there behind his friend. "Good morning! Come in, both of you," she said, swinging the door wide and moving aside to make room.

Ezak smiled and stepped into the house, with Kel following a step or two behind, but then he stopped so abruptly that Kel bumped into him, knocking him another step forward. Kel looked up at Ezak, startled. Ezak was staring at the room they had just entered. Kel looked around to see what had surprised him.

The room was large, taking up perhaps half the ground floor of the house, large enough that it needed two pillars to help support the ceiling, but Kel didn't think that was so very remarkable. There were two couches, and four armchairs, all upholstered in dark red; there were a few tables of various heights and sizes. The plank floor was mostly covered with an assortment of rugs, and the windows all had dark red drapes, which Kel supposed must be somewhat unusual out here in the country. The walls were largely hidden by shelves full of…full of *things*.

That must be what Ezak was staring at, Kel realized— the things on the shelves. And standing in the corners. And hanging from the ceiling on wires. Kel had no idea what the things *were*, though. They were a variety of colors, and came in thousand different shapes and sizes—the ones in the corners were there because they were too big to fit on any shelf, while others were so tiny they were stored in jars. Most of them were shiny, to one degree or another. Some were completely featureless, while others were covered with peculiar decorations and protrusions. None of them were familiar. The room smelled of oil, metal, and some spice Kel could not identify.

"Nabal…Nabal did well for himself, I see," Ezak said, a little hoarsely.

"Yes, he did," Dorna said, glancing around at the mysterious objects. "There are rather a lot of them, aren't there?"

Kel wanted to ask what they were talking about, but he resisted. That was the sort of question that could get him in trouble. He did not want to ruin Ezak's scheme, whatever it was.

"Yes," Ezak said.

"What brings you here this morning?" Dorna asked.

It took a moment for Ezak to tear his gaze from the shelves and reply, a delay long enough that Kel almost said something himself. He was deterred, though, by not knowing what to say—why *had* they come?

"Oh, we just wanted to offer our condolences, and to ask once more whether there is anything we can do to aid you in your time of sorrow."

"Ah," Dorna said. "As a matter of fact, I've been thinking about your offer."

Ezak swallowed. "Oh?"

"I don't think I need any advice; I can make up my own mind on most matters. If you really just want to be helpful, though—well, as you can see, my husband had a good many talismans. With Nabal gone, I don't think I want to stay here in the village; this was always more *his* home than mine, it isn't where I grew up, and everything here reminds me of him. I don't see any point in returning to my home village, either—my family there has all died or moved away, and after more than thirty years I doubt anyone else there even remembers me. I thought I might go to Ethshar of the Sands, instead, and buy myself a little tea shop there to keep myself busy. I'm very fond of tea. I can sell some of Nabal's magic to other sorcerers there to pay for it—there really isn't anyone around here who could buy them, but in Ethshar there are *dozens* of sorcerers. The thing is, all these talismans are a lot to move, and a woman traveling alone with valuables is at risk. If you really want to be helpful, perhaps you could assist me in transporting them, and accompany me to the city?" She smiled, and Kel reconsidered his opinion of her appearance—when she smiled, she was much prettier than he had realized.

"We'd be *delighted* to give you a hand," Ezak said, smiling back at her.

Kel didn't say anything. Carrying all that stuff looked like a lot of work, but at least it wasn't something that would get him in trouble. He wished Ezak would ask about maybe getting paid for it, though.

"How were you planning to move it all?" Ezak asked.

"Oh, I'll be buying a wagon," Dorna said.

"Ah," Ezak said, looking around.

"A *large* wagon," Dorna added.

"Indeed. I wonder whether perhaps dear Nabal had any sorcerous devices that might assist us in the task of moving—magical transport of some sort, or lifting devices? Perhaps I could take a look…?"

Dorna shook her head. "I think we'll do fine with our hands and an ordinary wagon."

Ezak bowed. "As you please." He smiled. "When will the wagon be available?"

She smiled again. "You seem very eager to get started."

"Ah, no! I am in no hurry, my dear. I merely wish to know how soon we must bid the delightful Irien farewell."

The smile vanished. "You know, she's the one thing here I think I'll miss. To the other villagers I was always the sorcerer's wife, someone to be honored and feared, someone you spent as little time with as possible. Irien, though…" She sighed. "Irien was my friend."

"Maybe she could come with you," Kel suggested.

Dorna blinked, startled, though Kel wasn't sure whether she was startled by the idea of Irien accompanying her, or the fact that Kel had spoken for the first time that morning.

"I'm sure she'd rather stay here," Ezak said, throwing Kel a dirty look. "After all, what would an innkeeper do without her inn? She can hardly bring it with her!"

"Maybe there's some magic that *would* let her bring it?" Kel ventured.

Dorna laughed. "Not that *I* know," she said.

"Don't be ridiculous, Kel," Ezak said. "Poor Nabal was the sorcerer here, and he's gone. There aren't any magicians left."

"Well, *you're* here," Dorna pointed out, aiming a thumb at Ezak.

"Yes, of course," Ezak said hastily. "I meant any *other* magicians. I'm afraid my modest skills are completely inadequate to the task of moving an inn. Besides, where would she *put* it? The streets of Ethshar of the Sands are full!"

Kel had no answer to that. Ezak was obviously right; in fact, the more Kel thought about it, the more foolish his suggestion seemed. Dorna was smiling at him, but at least she wasn't laughing outright. He ducked his head and looked around the room rather than meeting her eyes.

There really were a lot of things on the shelves, Kel thought. Were they *all* magic? If they were, that was a *lot* of sorcery. Even if Ezak did steal some of it, Dorna would still have plenty left, Kel told himself.

"I don't think Irien would want to bring her inn," Dorna said thoughtfully, "but she might want to come along all the same, if only to visit the city for a few days."

"Can she really afford to abandon her livelihood for that long?" Ezak asked.

"Oh, I'm sure something can be arranged." The sorcerer's widow considered for a moment, then said, "If you would excuse me, I believe I'll go speak to her right now. I hope you'll forgive me if I cut your visit short?"

"Oh, of course, of course!" Ezak forced a grin. "We'll get out of your way. Just let us know when we can be of service."

"You can walk with me to the inn, if you like."

Ezak bowed. "We would be honored."

Kel did not see that it was much of an honor, since all three of them would be going to the inn anyway, but he didn't say anything.

"If you could wait outside while I get my shawl?"

"Of course," Ezak said. He bowed again, but did not move toward the door until Kel tugged at his tunic.

"Come on," Kel murmured. He glanced at Dorna, who was looking both impatient and amused.

"I'm coming," Ezak said angrily, as he straightened.

A moment later the two men were standing outside the front door, waiting. Kel was content to stand there enjoying the warm morning air while he listened to a bird singing somewhere nearby, but Ezak leaned over and whispered, "Why did you suggest bringing the innkeeper along? The fewer eyes we have upon us, the better our chances of making a clean escape with all the sorcery we can carry!"

"Oh," Kel said. "I didn't think of that." He really hadn't been thinking about the mechanics of the planned theft at all.

"Did you *see* all those talismans?" Ezak said, jerking a thumb toward the door. "There are *hundreds* of them!"

"I guess so," Kel said. "I don't know what any of them are, though."

"Well, neither do I, not *specifically*, but so what? We can still sell them. I assume any sorcerer would recognize them, even if we don't. We'll be rich!"

Kel was not entirely convinced. He still remembered what that whip had felt like on his back, and Ezak had been sure that *that* scheme, selling phony spells to demonologists, would make them rich. Ezak had said that when the spells didn't work, the demonologists would just think they had made mistakes somewhere; he had never guessed that they could ask other demons whether the spells were real. Kel was very much afraid that he was making some similar mistake in this attempt to rob or swindle the sorcerer's widow. What if some of the talismans were used up or broken? What if *no one* knew what they were? This Nabal had apparently been a much better sorcerer than Kel would expect to find in a tiny village like this, if all those things were really magic.

Then there were all the lies Ezak had told. The more one lied, the more likely one was to be caught, in Kel's experience.

Kel didn't think Ezak's plan was going to work, but they were here, and Kel was sure that Ezak was smarter than Kel was even if he made mistakes sometimes. He thought up all *sorts* of plans, and some of them *did* work. Maybe not very *many*, but some.

Then the ash-streaked door opened and Dorna emerged, her soft blue shawl wrapped around her shoulders. Kel stepped back out of her way, while Ezak made an elaborate bow and moved as if to take her arm.

She did not accept his gesture; Kel thought she looked amused, or perhaps slightly annoyed. Instead she headed directly for the inn without pausing, leaving Ezak scrambling to follow.

Kel was not in any particular hurry, and it wasn't as if anyone was going very far. He took his time about following the other two, looking around the tiny village.

He could see why Dorna would not want to stay here. In fact, he didn't understand how a sorcerer had ever made a living here in the first place—or for that matter, how the blacksmith or the innkeeper managed it. There were no other people to be seen in the village itself, though he could see a few figures moving in the surrounding fields. Yes, a road ran through the village, but he didn't see anyone using it. Kel was a city boy, born and raised in the Smallgate district of Ethshar of the Sands, and he didn't really understand why anyone would want to live outside the city walls; how could you make a living without other people for customers? Besides, it seemed so *lonely* out here! Most of the time the loudest sound was birdsong; that seemed almost unnatural.

If Irien didn't want to come with them, Kel was sure Dorna could find plenty of new friends in Ethshar—but of course, old friends were the best. That was why Kel stayed with Ezak; they had been friends ever since they were boys, not yet wearing breeches. Ezak had protected Kel from the local bullies back on Barracks Street, and in exchange Kel had slipped into places where Ezak couldn't fit, and taken things Ezak wanted.

Ezak had also told stories about his Uncle Vezalis, the traveling merchant. Kel had met Uncle Vezalis, of course, but they did not get along very well, so he had heard about most of the adventures second-hand, from Ezak, and not directly from the source. Kel had happily listened to those stories, but he had never entirely believed them. Ezak liked to exaggerate, and Uncle Vezalis liked to exaggerate, so by the time a story had gone through both of them it might have grown like a mushroom after a rain. Kel knew he wasn't the smartest person around, but even *he* knew that some of the stories Ezak told him weren't true.

This time, though, if all those things really were magic, Ezak's uncle apparently hadn't exaggerated at all.

Kel glanced around, and wondered why Uncle Vezalis had ever come to this tiny little village in the first place. Had he come to trade with the sorcerer, or had this place just been on the way to somewhere else?

Then Kel was at the inn door, and Irien and Dorna were talking in the common room while Ezak listened unhappily.

"…eat on the way?" Irien was saying as Kel came within earshot.

Dorna laughed. "*You're* asking that? Irien, did you think you run the only inn between here and Ethshar?"

"No, no, of course not, but…Dorna, are you sure?"

"Sure I'm going, or sure you should come with me?"

"Both."

"Yes. To both."

"You know why Nabal stayed here."

"Yes, and I know I disagreed with him."

Kel glanced at Ezak, wondering whether he knew what the two women were talking about. Why *had* Nabal stayed here?

"That wasn't just bravado? I always thought you were… well, I didn't think you meant it. If you didn't want to stay here, why *did* you?"

Dorna turned up an empty hand. "Nabal was here," she said. Her voice cracked. "And now he's gone, so I'm leaving, and I'm asking if you'd like to come with me."

Irien looked up at the overhead beams, then back at the big stone hearth, then back at Dorna.

"I'll come," she said. "I may not stay there, though. I don't know whether I'll like the city, but I admit I'm curious to see it."

"Good enough!" Dorna said with a broad smile. "We'll leave as soon as my wagon is ready."

"It's two days to the cartwright in Balgant, and two days back, assuming he has one on hand. Four days, then?"

Ezak spoke up. "I would be happy to make that trip for you, if you like."

Dorna shook her head. "That won't be necessary. I'll send word right away. But I was thinking we might buy our wagons from farmers right here, and let *them* deal with the cartwright. I believe Grondar has one that would suit me."

"That's a good thought," Irien said.

"We could load tonight, and leave tomorrow morning."

"You *are* in a hurry! What about your house?"

"Anyone who wants it can have it."

Irien's expression turned grave. "Dorna, aren't you rushing a little? I know you've never been one to hesitate once your mind is made up, but are you *sure* you're so eager to abandon everything you've known for the last thirty years or more? This isn't your grief talking? Isn't there *anything* in the house you're sentimental about?"

"I'm sure, Irien. These two young men have dispelled any doubts I might have had—surely, their arrival is a sign from the gods."

Kel shifted uncomfortably and looked at Ezak, who gestured for silence.

"All right, then," Irien said. "I'll start packing, and we'll leave whenever you're ready."

"Good!" Dorna smiled. "I need to go take care of a few things." She turned and swept past Kel, back out of the inn and headed toward her own house.

Kel stepped aside as the widow passed, and watched her go. Now he turned back to find Ezak standing next to him.

Irien was nowhere to be seen, and had presumably gone to do the packing she had mentioned.

"Blast it," Ezak said. "She's coming with us."

Kel did not see that there was anything to be done about that, so he did not reply. Instead he said, "I don't think we're a sign from the gods."

Ezak, who had been staring at the departing Dorna, looked down at Kel. "What?"

"I don't think we're a sign from the gods," Kel repeated. "I don't *feel* like a sign."

"Don't be stupid," Ezak said. "How do you know what a sign feels like? But it doesn't matter what *you* think, anyway; what matters is that *she* thinks the gods sent us. If she does, then surely she'll trust us."

That seemed like something of a leap to Kel, but she could not say exactly where the flaw in his friend's logic was, so he did not say anything.

"Come on," Ezak said. "Let's go see what we can do to help." He marched out the door.

Kel followed.

THREE

Some of the local farmers were not happy to learn that the sorcerer's widow was leaving. Kel got the definite impression that while they might not have been her friends, they liked having her around. A sorcerer's presence was a point of pride for the tiny village, and even with the sorcerer gone, his widow was better than nothing. Her departure would reduce the place's prestige, such as it was.

Losing the innkeeper was another blow, though the inn itself obviously wasn't going anywhere. A few of the farm women made a point of questioning the smith to be sure he would not be following Dorna and Irien, as well.

Despite not wanting Dorna to leave, Grondar did not refuse to sell her his wagon—she had not wasted time haggling, but had simply offered him twice what he had paid the cartwright, in hard coin, and he could hardly turn *that* down! She had also paid twice the going rate for four oxen to haul it.

Another man, Hullod the Younger, had sold a wagon and a pair of oxen to Irien, though at a less generous price; Irien *did* haggle. Her resources, though vast compared to most of the locals, were far more limited than Dorna's.

But both sellers insisted on delaying delivery for a day, so that the village could give the two women a proper send-off. Other details arose, as well, and loading turned out to be a time-consuming task, as the sorcerous devices had to be handled with care, packed neatly and securely, and checked against their late owner's catalogue. As a result, it was a good four days later, after a reasonably lavish feast and far too much time sorting and packing, that Dorna's little caravan finally rolled out of the square, bound southeastward toward Ethshar.

Kel had said as little as possible, and had tried to be as helpful as possible, throughout the various preparations and the farewell party. He had kept a watchful eye on Ezak, and had sometimes whispered a warning to his companion when he thought the bigger man was doing something unwise.

That catalogue of talismans, for example—Ezak's interest in it had been far too obvious for Kel's liking.

"I *am* supposed to be a sorcerer," Ezak reminded him, when they were alone again. "Of course I'm interested in sorcery!"

"You looked more interested than that," Kel said.

Ezak glared at him. Then he said, "It doesn't matter anyway. I got a look at one page while she was checking it against the stuff we'd loaded, and I couldn't make any sense of it. I don't even know what language it's in."

Kel blinked. They might be days away from the city here, but they were still well inside the Hegemony of the Three Ethshars. "It isn't in Ethsharitic?"

Ezak shook his head. "The runes are Ethsharitic, but the words are gibberish. Those little blue things, shiny on one side and dark on the other? They're listed as *gob opo zishin*. That doesn't sound like *any* language I ever heard!"

"I guess sorcerers must have their own *secret* language," Kel said, as much to himself as to Ezak.

Other than the feast, which had been the best meal he had eaten in years, Kel's favorite part of the preparations was that in all the confusion Irien neglected to collect what Ezak and

Kel owed her for their stay at the inn. That was very welcome, since so far as Kel knew, they did not actually have the money. Ezak had spent what little coin they had when they arrived on assorted small purchases, in an attempt to make them look wealthy—after all, he was still pretending to be a sorcerer, and magicians always had money. Kel thought it would be far more convincing if he had actually demonstrated some sort of magic, but that was beyond Ezak's ability; his very limited skills in sleight of hand might possibly pass as minor wizardry, but bore no resemblance to any sorcery Kel had ever seen.

In the end the little company did get under way one cool still morning, with all the talismans loaded in the big open wagon Dorna had bought from Grondar, while the personal possessions of all four travelers were on the much smaller covered wagon Irien had bought from Hullod. A heavy yellow cloth was tied down over the sorcerous devices in Dorna's wagon, to keep them from bouncing out. Ezak expressed some concern about whether that would be sufficient in the event of rain, and Dorna almost laughed at him. "Didn't your master ever tell you that talismans are waterproof?" she asked.

"I don't recall that the subject ever came up," Ezak replied, a bit stiffly. He stalked over to the big wagon and climbed up onto the driver's bench.

Once they were moving out onto the road Irien took the lead with her wagon, with Kel riding beside her; Dorna and Ezak were in the rear, aboard the larger wagon.

They had been traveling for perhaps half an hour and had covered perhaps a mile in silence interrupted only by creaking wheels and an occasional bird when Kel finally said, "I'm sorry you aren't getting to ride with your friend."

Startled, Irien looked down at him. "I'll have plenty of time with her when we get to Ethshar," she said.

"Yes, but…well, then I'm sorry I'm not better company."

Irien snorted, and turned her attention back to the oxen. "I'd rather have you here than someone who's talking constantly."

Kel could not think of a good answer to that at first, but after a few more minutes he said, "Why aren't you riding with Dorna? Then you could talk to your friend. Ezak and I could drive one wagon, and you could drive the other."

Irien turned again to stare at him for a moment, then answered, "Do you really need to ask that?"

Confused, Kel leaned out to the side and looked back over his shoulder at Dorna and Ezak, on the driver's bench of the other wagon, then at Irien. "Yes," he said. "Why?"

Irien's mouth twisted up at one side. "Because we don't trust you, of course. What would stop you from driving away with one of our wagons?"

"Oh," Kel said. He thought for a moment, then said, "But you could chase us if we tried that."

"Your friend says he's a sorcerer; what if he has magic that can hobble our oxen?"

"But *you* could run faster than oxen! They're slow!"

"You might be surprised—oxen can run if they need to. But again, what if your friend has magic that can stop us?"

"I don't…" Kel stopped, trying to decide what he should say. Finally he simply turned up an empty palm and said nothing.

Two miles and another hour later, he asked, "Why are you letting us travel with you at all, if you don't trust us?"

Irien smiled at him. "If it was up to me, we wouldn't."

"Oh. Dorna wanted us to come?"

"Yes."

Kel considered that carefully, then asked, "Do you know why?"

Irien shifted in her seat, then said, "Because, she says, more hands make less work for each of us, and the sight of two men may make us a less tempting target for bandits than if we were two women alone. Not that there are a *lot* of bandits around here, but we've heard that a few have been seen in recent years." She grimaced. "Besides, she felt we owed it to you. I'm told that it was *your* idea for *me* to come, and Dorna wouldn't have asked me if you hadn't suggested it. She had originally planned to make the trip alone."

"By herself? That *would* be dangerous."

"Maybe," Irien said.

Half an hour later, Kel asked, "How did you become an innkeeper?"

Irien's answer took several minutes, and led to a long explanation of her family history—the short version was that she had inherited the place from her father's childhood friend. Kel kept encouraging her to continue adding details; Ezak always said that it was smart to let the other person talk. Not only might you learn something useful, but it would make them like you more, since people like talking about themselves and appreciate a good listener.

Also, if Irien was talking, Kel wasn't, and he wouldn't need to worry about saying anything he shouldn't. If she was talking about herself, she wouldn't be asking any awkward questions about Kel or Ezak.

Finally, the little caravan stopped for a rest and a meal, and as they stretched their legs Kel had a chance to talk to Ezak out of earshot of the two women.

"They don't trust us," he whispered.

"Oh? What makes you think that?"

"Because Irien *told* me they don't."

Ezak frowned. "Did she?"

"Yes. That's why they didn't ride together, so each one could keep an eye on one of us. They were worried that if we had one wagon to ourselves we might just drive off with it."

"That wasn't what Dorna said. She told me that she wanted to get to know me, since I'd known her husband long ago."

Kel had no answer for that.

"She asked me about my apprenticeship with Jabajag the Magnificent. She said Nabal never talked about him, so she was curious."

Kel blinked, then asked, "What sort of name is Jabajag?"

Ezak turned up a palm. "Who knows? A sorcerer's name, I suppose. At any rate, I talked myself hoarse, telling her stories about her husband's master, and about my career as a sorcerer in Ethshar, and about my family."

Kel chewed his lower lip apprehensively.

"Oh, don't look so worried, Kel!" Ezak said, slapping him on the back. "She believed every word, I'm sure! Not a bit of it was true, but she believed it all!"

"I hope so," Kel murmured.

"What did you tell the innkeeper? We want to keep our stories straight."

"Nothing," Kel said. "I let her do all the talking. I asked her how she became an innkeeper."

"Ah, excellent! Surprisingly clever of you, Kel!"

"You said that was smart. You said it was better to listen than to talk."

"That's right, I did, didn't I?" He laughed. "And very fine advice it was! Did you learn anything useful?"

"I don't know," Kel said. "Did you?"

Ezak's laughter stopped, and his frown reappeared. "No," he said. "She kept asking me questions, so I was too busy answering them to ask any of my own."

"Oh," Kel said.

"She might have become suspicious if I didn't answer."

"Oh," Kel said again.

For a moment both men were silent. Then Ezak said, "If they really don't trust us, then perhaps we should act swiftly, before they're ready."

"I don't understand."

"Well, they know we're from Ethshar, right? So they probably expect us to steal the big wagon once we're near the city, or even inside the walls. But if we were to steal it *tonight,* while they're asleep, when we're still days away from the city, they wouldn't be expecting it, and we could get a good start on them."

Kel considered this unhappily. "Maybe we shouldn't steal the wagon at all," he said.

Ezak started to wave this idea away, then stopped. "Hmmm," he said. "You know, we don't care about the *wagon* at all. We just want the magic. What if, while they're sleeping, we replace some of the talismans with worthless junk? We can hide the sorcery somewhere, then come back for it later."

That had not been what Kel meant, but he did not want to argue. Besides, Dorna had so *many* of those magical things; she could spare a few.

"*Hai!*" Irien called, interrupting their quiet conversation. "Are you two ready to go?"

"Just a moment!" Ezak called back. Then he leaned over and whispered to Kel, "You be ready tonight—don't go to sleep. Pretend if you have to."

"All right," Kel answered uncertainly.

"Excellent! Then let us be off!" He stood up and strode back toward the wagons.

Kel followed, and in moments they were back on the wagons, heading south. This time, though, Dorna suggested a change of partners, and Kel found himself riding in the larger second wagon with Dorna, while Ezak and Irien took the lead in the smaller wagon.

"So," Dorna said, once they were rolling, "tell me about yourself, Kelder of Ethshar."

Kel hesitated, then said, "There isn't much to tell."

"Oh, there must be. You're from Ethshar of the Sands?"

"Yes."

"From Morningside?"

Kel blinked in surprise. Morningside was one of the wealthiest districts, and although the tunic he wore had been a good one when it was new, he had thought its shabby, worn condition, along with his lack of a hat or other accessories, would make it clear that he was not rich. "No," he said.

"Where, then?"

"Smallgate." Desperate to change the subject before he gave anything away, he added, "Are you from that village?" He gestured back over his shoulder.

"Me? No."

"Where are you from, then?"

"Oh, another village."

"What village? What was its name?"

"We called it Gaffrir."

"Is that a Northern name?"

It was Dorna's turn to hesitate. "I don't know," she said.

"It doesn't sound Ethsharitic."

"No, it doesn't, does it? Not like Smallgate." She smiled at him. "Tell me about Smallgate."

Kel looked around at the countryside, at the blue sky and green fields and tidy white and brown farmhouses, hoping for inspiration, then turned up a palm. "It's just like any part of the city, I suppose—streets and houses and shops."

"You've lived in Smallgate all your life?"

"More or less." He looked down at the footboard, wishing she would change the subject.

"Did you serve your apprenticeship there?"

Kel turned to stare at her. "Apprenticeship? *I* never served an apprenticeship."

"You didn't?"

"No!"

"But I thought Ezak said…"

Kel shook his head vigorously. "I was never an apprentice. If Ezak told you otherwise he was joking. He does that, sometimes—makes jokes. I don't always understand them. They aren't usually very funny."

Dorna smiled. "No? *I* think he's funny."

"You're smarter than I am."

Dorna seemed to consider that for a moment before saying, "Tell me about your family."

"Don't have one," Kel answered, looking away. "Ma died when I was eight."

"What about your father, or your grandparents?"

"I don't have any, so far as I know."

"Is that why you never served an apprenticeship?"

"That, and other things. I didn't especially want one." That was not entirely true, but he did not care to discuss his background with the sorcerer's widow.

"No? You didn't want to be a sorcerer, like your friend Ezak?"

Kel spread empty hands.

"Did you ever have any brothers or sisters?" Dorna asked.

"Don't know. Did you?"

"I have a younger sister. I haven't seen her in years."

"Why not?"

"Because…well, she doesn't live around here."

"What about your parents? Are they back in Gaffrir?"

"No. My father's dead, and my mother went home to *her* parents, in Aldagmor."

"So you do have grandparents?"

Dorna shook her head. "No," she said. "At least, I don't think so, not anymore. But they were still alive when my father died."

Kel nodded.

They rode on in silence for a few minutes, then Dorna asked, "How did you meet Ezak?"

"Don't remember," Kel said.

"You don't?"

"We were little."

"Oh. So you've been friends all your lives?"

Kel nodded. "Our mothers were friends. He looked after me after my mother died."

"So you went with him when he was apprenticed?"

Kel knew that Ezak's real apprenticeship, to a potter, had lasted all of a sixnight before Ezak's master threw him out for stealing, but he knew Dorna meant Ezak's imaginary training in sorcery. He certainly wasn't going to try to tell a bunch of complicated lies about that that might or might not match Ezak's; instead he told one simple half-truth. "No," he said. "I stayed in Smallgate and looked after myself. I was bigger by then."

"So Ezak came back and found you when he was a journeyman?"

"Yes."

"So what do you do for a living? Are you his assistant?"

"No. We're just friends. I do odd jobs. What about you?"

Dorna stared at him for a moment, then laughed. "I'm a housewife," she said. "Though I did help Nabal look after his things."

Kel gestured at the wagon. "So you know what all those things back there do?"

Dorna hesitated. "Some of them," she said.

Kel knew this was his opportunity to learn something *really useful*, to find out what some of the talismans did, and maybe which ones would be most worth stealing, but he couldn't think of how to phrase a useful question. Talking to Dorna wasn't like talking to Irien; it had been easy to get Irien talking about herself, about innkeeping, and about her family, but Dorna didn't seem to want to say much. Her answers seemed short and uninformative—just as Kel tried to keep his own answers. She kept asking him new questions, instead of saying more about herself.

Ezak was going to be disappointed if Kel wasted a chance to find out more about sorcery, but he just could not come up with a good lead-in. And after all, it wasn't as if Ezak had done all that well himself.

Finally, Kel just said, "Oh?"

"Some of them," Dorna repeated. Then she leaned back on the wagon-bench and looked at the road ahead, ignoring Kel.

They rode most of the rest of the afternoon in silence.

FOUR

Kel was embarrassed to realize, when Ezak's shaking awoke him, that he had dozed off. He lay propped against a wagon-wheel in the night-shrouded stableyard behind the Golden Rooster, the only inn in the village of Shepherd's Well, and until he started out of his slumber his head had been slumped on his shoulder.

He and Ezak were outdoors in the chilly dark, instead of inside the nice warm inn, because they had not had the money to do otherwise. They had claimed they were going to take turns guarding the wagons, to explain why they didn't take a room; Ezak did not want to admit they couldn't *afford* a room.

Dorna and Irien, of course, had taken a room. At the time Kel had not seen anything odd about that, but now, as he sat up and looked around in the dark, he wondered about it. Irien had told him that the women didn't trust them, so why had they been allowed to stay out here with the wagons? Something didn't feel right about that.

"Come on," Ezak said. "Get up. I want your help with this."

"With what?" Kel asked, struggling to see his surroundings. Ezak was holding a shuttered lantern, and the stars were out, but neither moon was visible, leaving most of the yard in deep shadow.

"This mounting block."

"This what?"

"This mounting block! Come on, sleepyhead!"

It took Kel a moment to remember what a mounting block was—a big block of wood or stone that a young or otherwise undersized rider could stand on to make it easier to climb onto a horse. When he did recall it, he asked, "What do you want a mounting block for? I didn't see any horses."

"There aren't any horses. I intend to swap it for that big boxy thing in the sorcerer's collection."

Kel remembered the device, or talisman, or whatever it was, that Ezak was referring to. The second-largest of all the magical objects Dorna had loaded into the wagon, it was mostly made of something that gleamed like silver, but was not quite the right color for silver. It was more or less rectangular, but had several odd ribs protruding along its long sides, and dozens, maybe hundreds, of little square inlays in every color of the rainbow were set into its smooth top. "Why?" Kel asked. "What does that one do?"

"I haven't the slightest idea, but Kel, a hunk of magic that big must be worth a fortune! If we can get it out, and put the mounting block in its place, the sorcerer's widow will never know it's gone. We can bury it or hide it somewhere and come back for it later."

Kel hesitated. "Wouldn't it be safer to steal a few little ones?"

"It might be safer, but it wouldn't be as profitable. Come on, Kel, give me a hand."

With a sigh, Kel got to his feet and followed the dim glow of the lantern to the corner where the mounting block sat. There he and Ezak stooped down, each of them taking one side of the stone block, and lifted.

It came up easily. "It's not as heavy as it looks," Kel said.

"Heaving it over the side of the wagon without smashing anything is the hard part," Ezak said. "Come on."

Carrying the block between them, they made their way back to Dorna's wagon, where they paused. "Put it down," Ezak said. "I'll get the talisman out, and then we'll put the block in its place."

"All right," Kel said. He and Ezak set the block down, and then Kel stepped back and watched as his friend climbed up into the wagon. He saw Ezak open the lantern shutters a little so that he could see his surroundings more clearly, then set the lantern down on the driver's bench.

Then Ezak started untying the ropes that secured the canvas cover that protected the contents of the wagon, and a sense of foreboding crawled up Kel's back and seemed to pull his shoulders inward. "Ezak?" he called.

"Sssh!" Ezak replied. "I'm trying to find...ah, there it is!" He flung back a corner of the canvas, then reached down into the wagon.

A high-pitched, inhuman voice screamed, very loudly, and kept screaming. Kel clapped his hands over his ears and turned to look at the door of the inn, expecting to see a dozen armed guards spilling out.

No one emerged; the inn remained quiet and dark. Meanwhile, Ezak was saying, "Hush! Shut up! Stop it!" He was bent down, his hands flailing wildly at something Kel could not see.

Then the screaming stopped, as abruptly as it had begun. Kel blinked, his ears ringing. "What was *that*?" he asked. His words sounded very faint in his own ears, in marked contrast to the unearthly wail that had just ended.

"I don't know," Ezak said. "It started when I touched the...the whatever-it-is, so I thought maybe I could make it stop the same way, so I just kept hitting it—"

An unfamiliar voice interrupted him, and Kel and Ezak both stopped talking as this new voice said half a dozen incomprehensible words, then fell silent.

For a moment after it finished no one spoke, but at last Kel asked, "What was *that*?"

"The...it's the same thing," Ezak replied. "The big talisman."

"What did it say?"

"I don't know," Ezak said. "I don't even know what *language* that was."

"Ezak, how can a talisman talk? It doesn't even have a mouth!"

"I know. I mean, I know it doesn't have a mouth, I don't know how it can talk. I didn't see anything move, but I'm sure that's where the voice came from."

"But how?"

"Magic, of course," Ezak said, regaining some of his confidence. "It must be sorcery. *That* should bring a good price!"

"Why? We don't know what it said!"

"Well, if we find someone who *does*—"

The talisman spoke again. Kel thought it repeated the exact same words it had said before, and once again, when it had completed its single sentence it stopped.

"Maybe that's all it knows how to say," Kel said. "That's not very impressive. I saw a wizard do something like that once; he made a mouth appear on a piece of cloth and say six words. But they weren't words in any known language, and the wizard's apprentice told me it always said the same six words, but not always in the same order."

"Maybe," Ezak said. He was leaning over, staring down at the talisman. "But some of those little squares on the top are glowing. Blue ones."

Kel hesitated, torn between curiosity and caution. "Do you think it's safe? It won't…turn us into lizards, or something?"

"How should *I* know?" Ezak said. "But it hasn't hurt us yet, and I was whacking it all over when it was screaming at us." He reached over the side of the wagon, and tapped the big talisman.

There was a sudden clatter, and Ezak jumped back, falling off the bench and tumbling awkwardly over the wagon's tongue to the ground. Kel started to run to his friend's aid, then froze where he was and stared.

The talisman was climbing out of the wagon. The ribs on its sides had unfolded into black-clawed, spider-like legs, and it was pulling itself up over the wooden side. It looked utterly monstrous in the dim light and deep shadows, the orange lantern light gleaming from its metallic sides while a faint blue glow shone from its top, and Kel had to clamp his jaw to keep from screaming.

When he trusted himself to speak, he exclaimed, "Ezak, what did you *do*?"

"How should *I* know?" Ezak said, lying sprawled where he had fallen. He pushed himself up on one elbow and watched as the thing lowered itself to the ground, hanging by two of its many legs until three or four of the others were solidly braced on the hard-packed earth. Both men fell silent and merely watched, unmoving, as the talisman, or creature, or whatever it was, arranged itself on earth of the stableyard.

Kel counted twelve legs, each ending in several fingers—not the same number on each, nor for that matter the same shape. Some were big crablike claws, others were long needles, and others were a variety of other shapes he could not make out clearly. He was not entirely sure of the number of legs; he thought the low light might be hiding one or two more.

Then the thing spoke again, still in that unknown language but different words, and then it began running. It did not run like a spider, or like anything else Kel had ever seen; its legs seemed to dance, and then it was moving.

It moved *fast*. Before Kel could really get a good look at it, it was out the stableyard gate into the night.

Startled, not thinking about any danger, Kel ran after it, but quickly gave up—it was already a good fifty yards away, visible only as a cluster of faint glowing blue dots vanishing down the road in the distance. He turned back, and saw that the inn door was open. A woman was standing there, holding a lantern—and looking at him.

He hung his head, but did not attempt to hide, or pretend he did not know why she was there. He could not see her face in the dark—she was not holding the lantern in such a way as to illuminate it—but he judged from her height that it was Dorna, rather than Irien. He walked slowly back to the inn.

She stood in the doorway and watched, and when he had drawn close enough that she had no need to shout, she said, "Which one was it?"

He blinked. "What?"

"Well, judging by the sound, someone disturbed some of Nabal's magic, and here you are, Kel, looking as if you were chasing something but couldn't catch it. I'm guessing that one of the talismans woke up and flew off somewhere. Which one was it?"

"It didn't fly," Kel said. "It ran." She stepped out of the doorway, and he noticed that she was fully dressed, in a good green dress; that was probably why she had not come running out sooner.

Her tone, which had been fairly casual, turned more serious. "Damn," she said. "Which one?"

"I don't know what it's called," Kel said. He held out his hands about a foot and a half apart. "It was about this big, and it grew a dozen legs and crawled out of the wagon and ran away."

"Did it have lots of little colored squares on top?" Dorna asked. She sounded worried now.

"Yes," Kel said. "Some of them were glowing."

"Oh, *blast*! Why did it have to be that?" She seemed to be talking to herself, but then her attention returned to Kel. "Glowing yellow? Or red?" He could hear tension in her voice.

"No; blue."

"Just blue? *All* of them were blue?"

"Yes. Well, all the glowing ones."

"Oh." She relaxed slightly. "That's not so bad, then."

"It's not?"

"No." She held up the lantern and peered about at the empty road and the sleeping village. "I don't know how in the World you woke it up as safely as that, though."

"*I* didn't touch it!" Kel protested, before he realized what he was doing.

She turned to look at him. "Oh," she said. "It was Ezak?"

"I don't know," Kel mumbled, looking down at his feet.

"Oh, of course you do," Dorna replied. "Huh. If he managed to properly wake up a *fil drepessis*, maybe he really *is* a sorcerer. Where is he?"

"I don't know," Kel said—more or less truthfully, this time.

"He's still in the stableyard, isn't he? Probably stuffing talismans in his pouch." She sighed. "Come on."

Kel followed her as she marched through the gate into the stableyard.

Ezak was nowhere to be seen, but that did not surprise Kel; his friend was good at hiding. Kel thought Ezak might still be there, concealed in some dark corner, or he might have fled, but at any rate he was not sitting on the wagon, or standing in front of it.

Dorna stamped across the yard to the wagon and held the lantern up above her head, lighting the immediate area, but Ezak was still not visible.

"Idiot," she muttered. Then she climbed up on the driver's bench step and looked down into the wagon, poking at the flung-back cover and shoving some of the talismans about. She fumbled with one about the size of a dinner plate, then set that aside and pulled out a golden object roughly the size and shape of a man's boot-heel. "Here we go," she said.

"We do?" Kel asked.

"Yes, we do," she said, looking at the thing in her hand. "Kel, go inside and tell Irien I need to talk to her."

"But it's the middle of the night!"

Dorna looked up and turned to glare at him. "Do you think *anyone* is still asleep after all that noise?"

"Oh," Kel said. "Probably not."

"Then go get Irien."

Kel went.

He found Irien, the innkeeper, and the innkeeper's son sitting at a table in the common room, looking half-asleep— but only half. A single thick candle burned in the center of the table, lighting their faces, so Kel could see their expressions; they did not seem pleased to be there. They looked up as he stepped in, but did not say anything.

"Dorna wants to talk to you, Irien," Kel said. "She's in the stableyard."

Irien stood up, and looked as if she was about to say something, but then thought better of it and simply marched out the door, shoving past Kel without a word.

Kel hesitated, gave the other two a quick glance, called, "I'm sorry we disturbed you," then followed her out.

Dorna was still in the stableyard, but now had a large canvas bag slung over one shoulder, and was carefully choosing talismans from the wagon and putting them in the bag. She looked up.

"Good, you're back," she said to Kel, before turning to her friend and saying, "Irien, these fools have sent one of my husband's devices rampaging about the countryside, and I'm going to go retrieve it. I would very much appreciate it if you could stay here and watch our belongings until I return."

"How long will that be?" Irien asked.

"How should *I* know?" Dorna snapped. Kel cringed at the anger in her voice.

Irien frowned. "Right. I hope it won't be too long."

"It shouldn't be. I can track the *fil drepessis* with this." She held up the boot-heel thing.

Irien nodded. "When are you leaving?"

"Immediately," Dorna answered. "If we're very lucky, we may be able to catch it quickly and be back in a few hours."

"We?" Irien looked at Kel.

"Yes, 'we.' I'm taking Kel and Ezak with me, to make sure they don't cause any more trouble."

"You are?" Kel said, startled.

"Yes, I am. Now, go fetch Ezak out of the tack room, grab those packs of yours, and let's get going."

"Tack room?"

"Over there," Dorna said, pointing at a door in the corner of the stableyard that Kel had not really noticed before. "You really didn't know where he hid?"

"I really didn't," Kel said. "How did *you* know?"

"Sorcery. Now, get him out here, and let's get moving. You interrupted my sleep, and I'm not going to be able to get back to bed for some time, so I don't have much patience for your stupidity."

"Sorcery?"

"Just get him out here!"

Kel ran for the tack room door.

The little room beyond was dark and smelled strongly of leather and oil; Kel peered into the gloom, trying to make out what was inside. As his eyes, already used to the night, adjusted, he saw walls hung with oxbows and harnesses— and sure enough, Ezak was crouching in a corner, behind a rack holding a couple of saddles.

Ezak held a finger up to his lips.

Kel hesitated.

Dorna called from behind, "Tell Ezak that he *really* doesn't want me to come in there after him. My late husband provided me with magical weapons to protect myself when he was away, and I have one of them in my hand right now."

"Did you hear that?" Kel whispered.

Ezak sighed. "I heard," he said, getting to his feet. "You know, if you had told her I wasn't in here, instead of whispering to me, she might have believed you."

"Oh," Kel said. "I didn't think of that."

"I know," Ezak said. "You never do." He straightened his tunic, lifted his chin, and said, "Come on. Let's get this over with."

FIVE

"I still don't understand it," Ezak murmured to Kel, glancing at Dorna as she marched through the green wheat fields a few yards ahead of them. They had left the road about a mile back and were marching northeastward cross-country, following the sorcerer's widow. The weather had warmed up, but it was still a pleasant spring day. "How is she *doing* this?"

"Doing what?" Kel asked.

Ezak swept a hand across the World, from the golden dawn in the east to the lesser moon peeping through drifting wisps of fog to the west. "All of it!" he said. "How did she know where I was, back at the inn? How does she know where that thing went? How does she know what it *is*? A...a fill trespasses, or whatever she said."

"Magic," Kel said. It seemed perfectly obvious to him, and she had *said* she used sorcery to find Ezak's hiding place.

"But how can *she* work magic? Her *husband* was a sorcerer; *she* isn't."

"He must have taught her."

"But why would he *do* that?"

Kel turned up an empty palm. "I guess because he loved her."

"What does *that* have to do with it?" Ezak shook his head. "Magic is supposed to be *secret*. Magicians only reveal the secrets to their apprentices, not their families."

Kel had no answer.

"Or maybe," Ezak said, as if suddenly coming to a great realization, "she *is* a sorcerer. Maybe they were *both* sorcerers. Maybe that's why he married her!" He stared at Dorna with new interest.

Kel was not concerned with this theorizing. Obviously, Dorna *did* know something of sorcery; what did it matter *how* she knew it? No one was surprised when the baker's wife made delicious cookies, or when the weaver's husband could tell good cloth from bad; why should it be a surprise that a sorcerer's widow knew something about sorcery?

A thought struck him. "If she's a sorcerer, why would she want to open a tea shop?"

"She wouldn't," Ezak said. "She must have said that to trick us."

"Trick us into what?"

"I don't know," Ezak said, frowning.

Kel did not say anything more, but he did not think Dorna was a sorcerer. He thought she had picked up a little of her husband's knowledge, nothing more, and really did intend to open a tea shop, but he knew he had no evidence for this that would convince Ezak.

And Ezak *did* have evidence that she was a magician, in the form of Dorna herself, leading them through the fields with that little golden thing in her hand. Kel had gotten a glimpse of the glyphs on its gently-glowing surface and had been unable to make any sense of them, but he could barely read ordinary Ethsharitic, let alone any sort of magical symbols, so that didn't mean much. He thought he had heard it murmuring, but he hadn't been able to make out any words, or tell what language they were. Obviously, the thing was a sorcerer's talisman, but Kel didn't believe that meant only a sorcerer could use it. He had seen people back in Ethshar using magical items they had bought—protective runes, animated teapots, and the like—without anyone assuming they were magicians, and this just seemed like more of the same. Presumably Dorna's husband had shown her how to use the boot-heel talisman at some point, just as the magicians who created those other things had shown their customers how to use them.

"Why does she have us following her, anyway?" Ezak asked. "What good are we going to be when she finds that thing?"

"*I* don't know," Kel said. "Why don't you *ask* her?"

Ezak gave him that familiar frustrated glower that Kel knew meant "You really *are* an idiot, aren't you?" Kel had long ago stopped letting it bother him, especially since some time back he had noticed that it often turned out, when Ezak did that, that in fact Kel was right and Ezak was wrong. He had never been enough of an idiot to point *that* out to Ezak, though.

This time he really didn't think he was being foolish. In a sudden burst of determination, he ran forward, before Ezak could stop him, and said, "Excuse me, Dorna?"

She looked up from her talisman. "Yes?"

"Why are we here?"

She glanced back at Ezak, then looked Kel in the eye as they continued through the wheat. The two of them were roughly the same height, their eyes on a level, so this did not take any great effort. "Who is 'we'?"

"Me. Ezak. If you really just wanted us to stay out of trouble you could have chased us off, or turned us over to a magistrate."

"If I thought that would *work*, I might have—but you caused this problem, so it's only fair you help me fix it."

"You want us to help you with the…escaped thing?"

"Yes." Her tone left no doubt that she meant it, and would not tolerate a refusal.

"But how? *We* don't know…" He stopped in mid-sentence; he had been about to tell her that they didn't know anything about magic, but at the last second he had remembered that Ezak was pretending to be a sorcerer.

"Don't know what?"

"What you want us to do to help you," he finished weakly.

She smiled. "Well, if we do have to catch the *fil drepessis* by force, it'll be easier if we can surround it, so it can't dodge."

"Oh," Kel said. That made perfect sense to him.

"Besides," Dorna added, the smile vanishing, "I don't think Shepherd's Well *has* a magistrate, and there certainly wasn't one I'd trust. I wasn't about to leave the two of you back there with someone you might talk into helping you steal a wagonload of magic."

"Steal?" Kel squeaked.

"Yes, steal. You can't possibly still think you're fooling me after you set the *fil drepessis* off, can you?"

Kel didn't answer; he simply looked miserable.

Dorna stopped walking and turned to glare at him. "I knew you were frauds when we first met, when Ezak—if that's really his name—said he and Nabal were apprentices together," she said. "Not very *bright* frauds, either—I mean, leaving aside the fact that from the look of it Ezak wasn't *born* yet when Nabal was a journeyman, did you really think I didn't know my husband's master? Didn't know all his apprentices?"

"I don't know," Kel whispered, eyes cast down.

"Nabal's master was my *father*. That's how we met. You two really should have done your research more carefully."

"Oh," Kel said. After a moment, he asked, "His name wasn't really Jabajag, then?"

"Of course not. I just made up the stupidest name I could think of to see whether Ezak would guess I was onto him. My father's name was Arnen Azdaram's son. He didn't need some silly pompous name like Jabajag the Magnificent; he wasn't some stupid wizard trying to impress his customers, he was a great sorcerer, an Initiate of the Inner Mysteries!"

She sounded furious, and Kel did not blame her. He and Ezak had made fools of themselves, trying to trick her, and she had every right to be angry with them.

But then she continued, "Nabal was his last and best apprentice, who inherited all my father's magic, and you two thought you could...could just take it?" Her voice cracked, and Kel looked up to see tears in her eyes. "You wouldn't know what to do with any of it! You probably can't tell a *tokka* from a *noog*. How *dare* you?"

"I'm sorry," Kel said. He realized, a bit belatedly, that she wasn't really upset with *him*; she was grieving. She had seemed so calm, so controlled, since they first met her that he had almost forgotten she had lost her husband just a few days ago. Now her control had slipped a little.

"You're lucky I didn't just blow you both to bloody bits," she said, her voice wild. "I *could*, you know. I'm no sorcerer, I never apprenticed with my father or anyone else, but I've lived my whole life around sorcery. Even when I was a little girl, my father had to teach me which talismans were which so I could help him in his workshop without hurting myself. I know how to use a *zir* or a *shokkun*, and the wagon back at the inn is full of them."

"I don't know what those are," Kel said.

"Of course you don't!" she shouted. "Because you're a dirty little sneak thief, not a sorcerer or a sorcerer's wife."

"Maybe we should just go away and leave you alone," he said.

"Oh, no! Oh, no, you don't. You two set the *fil drepessis* off, and you're going to help me get it back! It's worth almost as much as the rest of that wagon put together."

Kel blinked. "It is?"

"Yes, it is! And while he obviously didn't know my father, maybe that friend of yours really *does* know some sorcery, since he woke it up."

"I...I don't think so," Kel said, glancing at Ezak, who was pointedly not listening.

"Well, even if he doesn't, the *fil drepessis* responded to him, so I might need him to get it back, so you're coming with me until we find it." She was starting to regain control, Kel saw; she wiped the tears from one cheek.

"I don't understand," Kel said, "but I'll try to help."

She glared at him for a moment, then turned to glower at Ezak, who was standing thirty or forty feet away, trying to look unconcerned, as if he stood out in the middle of a wheat field every day. "What about him?"

"I don't know," Kel said. "I can't tell Ezak what to do."

"Well, you can tell him that if he *doesn't* help, I'll hunt him down and kill him. I can find him anywhere."

"I'll tell him," Kel promised.

"Then go do it," Dorna said, with a wave of her hand. "I'll wait here."

Kel nodded, then turned and ran to Ezak.

"What happened?" Ezak asked. "What does she want? What did she get so angry about?"

"She wants us to help her find that thing that ran off—and she knows we came to steal from her. Her husband's master wasn't named Jabajag. She said that to test you, and you failed."

"What? But why did she... Why was she testing us?"

"I don't know," Kel lied.

"That's what she's mad about?"

"That, and her husband dying, and that thing running off."

Ezak nodded. There was a calculating look in his eye that Kel did not like.

"She says it's worth almost as much as the rest of the wagon put together, and if you don't help her get it back she'll hunt you down and kill you. She isn't a sorcerer, but her husband taught her how to use some of his magic." Kel did not want to say anything about Dorna's father, though he wasn't sure why not. "She says she may need you to catch it because you were the one who set it off."

Ezak nodded again, then hesitated. "What is this thing we're looking for?" he asked. "What does it do? Why is it so valuable?"

"I don't know," Kel said. "You could ask her."

"Did she threaten to kill you? She threatened to kill *me*."

"No, she didn't threaten me. Just you."

"*You* ask her, then!"

"We'll both ask," Kel said. "Please?"

Ezak grimaced. "Oh, all right," he said.

Together, the two men walked over to where Dorna stood. "Kel tells me," Ezak said, "that you demand I help you catch this escaped talisman."

"That's right. You started it, so you'll help me catch it, or I'll rip your heart out."

"He also said that you don't believe I'm a sorcerer."

"I don't," Dorna said. "You might be a failed apprentice, I suppose, but mostly you're a thief." When Ezak started to open his mouth again, she snapped, "Don't bother to argue! Do you think I can't tell a lie from the truth?"

Kel could see from his expression that in fact, Ezak did *not* think she could tell lies from truth, but he apparently had more sense than to say so.

"Oh, don't try to look innocent," Dorna said. "I told your friend Kel that I was a housewife, but I was also the village magistrate. I know a liar and a thief when I see one."

"Fine," Ezak said petulantly. "I'm not really a sorcerer."

"I'm glad you admit it. Go on, then—what were you going to say?"

"I don't know what this thing is that we're following, so I don't know how I can help. What *is* it? What does it do?"

"I told you, it's a *fil drepessis*."

"But what does that *mean*? What does it do? If you tell us, we might be able to help more easily."

She considered that for a moment, then sighed. "I don't know what the words mean," she said. "As for what it does, it finds sorcery that doesn't work anymore, and fixes it."

"It…does?" Ezak blinked in surprise.

"It does. And *you*, Ezak, apparently told it to go find a particular kind of sorcery and fix it. But we don't know what kind. The blue glow means it knew where to look, so it should eventually find whatever it is, and that it knows how to fix it. Can you tell me what you did to it? That might help."

Ezak glanced at Kel, who kept his mouth tightly shut. Ezak sighed.

"I put my hand on it, and it started screaming, so I started hitting it, trying to make it stop," Ezak admitted. "Then a bunch of the little blue squares lit up, and it began talking to me."

"What did it say?" Dorna demanded.

"I don't know," Ezak said. "It wasn't Ethsharitic."

"Of course it wasn't! Sorcery always speaks in the secret languages, never anything anyone human still uses. What did it *sound* like?"

Ezak looked helplessly at Kel, then said, "I don't know."

Dorna turned to Kel. "Did *you* hear it?"

"I guess so," Kel said. "It sounded sort of like... Skin specks fie die ten, maybe?"

"That's no help. If it said what I think it did, it told you it was going hunting, but unless there was more to the message than that, it didn't say where, or what it was looking for."

"I don't remember any more than that," Kel said unhappily.

"Dorna?" Ezak said.

She turned to glare at him.

"How...how can it know what to do?" Ezak said. "How to fix anything? It's just a...a device! I never heard of such a thing!"

"Of course you didn't, idiot!" Dorna snapped. "It's a *secret*, like most sorcery! And besides, it's no surprise you never heard of anything like it; that may be the last *fil drepessis* in the World. It's been handed down from master to apprentice for at least three hundred years. It's why we were living out in the middle of nowhere, instead of somewhere civilized; Nabal didn't want to have every other sorcerer in Ethshar demanding his help fixing old talismans. It's how we had so *much* magic—he used it to find, fetch, and fix all the old talismans for a dozen leagues in every direction. There was fighting in this area on and off all through the Great War, sorcerers were active here for *centuries*, so there were a *lot* of talismans."

"Oh," Kel said. Several things suddenly made more sense.

"But…it fixes broken magic?" Ezak said. "How can magic break?"

"Oh, that's *easy*," Dorna said. "Listen, what do you boys know about magic?"

The two exchanged glances, and Ezak gestured for Kel to go ahead. *He* didn't want to admit his ignorance, but if Kel did, that was fine.

"Hardly anything," Kel said.

"Well, magic is all about power," she said. "Come on, I'll explain as we walk—we don't want the *fil drepessis* to get any further ahead." She turned and began marching on through the wheat, following the thing's track with her magical golden boot-heel, and the two young men hurried to keep up with her.

"So," she said, as they walked, "magic is about using power to do things that don't happen naturally, and the different kinds of magic all use different kinds of power. Witchcraft uses the power of the witch's own body, but using it through the spirit, instead of by moving muscle and bone. Theurgists use the power of gods, and demonologists use the power of demons. Wizards use the raw chaos that exists everywhere outside our universe; they let little bits of it leak in, and they channel it with spells. And sorcerers do the opposite of wizards—they use the order that underlies the World, the patterns inside everything. Sorcerers make talismans that channel the nature of our reality into doing what they want. If you take exactly the right metals and crystals and things, and assemble them into exactly the right pattern, the right talisman, then it channels the energy of the World itself, an energy we call *gaja*, and that makes magic happen. You understand?"

Kel and Ezak exchanged glances. "I think so," Ezak said warily.

"Well, if something changes the pattern, however slightly, then it won't channel power properly anymore. A talisman is just crystals and metal arranged correctly, and if anything happens to disrupt that arrangement, it stops working. Sometimes just dropping one is enough to break it. It may not *look* broken, the damage is usually too small to see, but it stops working. What the *fil drepessis* does is find where the pattern is broken, and put everything back the way it should be. Then the talisman will work again."

"Can't a sorcerer fix his own talismans?"

She turned up an empty palm. "Sometimes," she said. "If he knows the pattern and can find where it's broken. But a lot of talismans are old, left from long ago, and no one remembers exactly how some of them are made. Some talismans can be made from scratch by anyone who knows how, but others... well, sometimes you need one talisman to make another, and maybe that one took another, which needed another, back through dozens of them. Sorcery may well be the oldest form of magic; whether it is or not, it's certainly been around for thousands of years, and there have been hundreds of generations of talismans. A sorcerer may not have the talismans he needs to make the talismans he needs to make the talisman he wants. He may not even know which talismans he needs."

"But the full-drapes-hiss knows?" Ezak asked.

Dorna nodded. "Yes," she said. "That's its magic."

Kel pointed at the boot-heel device. "That's metals and crystals arranged a particular way?"

"Yes."

"It looks like a boot-heel."

Dorna looked at the talisman, and gave a snort of laughter. "I suppose it does," she said.

"Boot-heels are made of wood or leather. Could you make a talisman of wood or leather?"

Dorna shook her head. "No," she said. "The structures in wood and leather and just about anything else that comes from living things aren't regular enough to make the right patterns. Sorcerers can only work with absolutely pure metals and crystals, and they have to be the *right* metals and crystals. You can't substitute tin for copper, or iron for lead, or beryl for garnet."

"But *wizards* use living things," Kel protested.

"Wizards are working with chaos. Sorcerers work with order."

Kel did not find that entirely convincing, but he let it drop and brought up another objection. "I didn't see patterns in some of the things in the wagon."

"The patterns are usually too fine to be seen with the naked eye. That's one reason you need talismans to make more talismans."

Ezak spoke up again. "That's all very interesting," he said, "but tell us more about the full-drapes-hiss."

"*Fil drepessis*," Dorna corrected him.

"Whatever. You said I woke it up and told it do do something?"

"Yes. It's all patterns—to give it instructions, you tap the top of it, and the pattern of tapping tells it what you want it to do. I deliberately left it in a half-awake state where if someone touched it without a pattern, it would scream—that was to keep away thieves. Like you. I thought that would be enough to scare you away, but apparently I misjudged. You must have accidentally made a good pattern when you were hitting it, but we don't know which one, so we don't know what it's looking for."

"How do sorcerers know what patterns to make?"

Dorna grimaced. "*That*, dear boy, is what sorcerers need a nine-year apprenticeship to learn."

"But *you* know how to use that boot-heel!" Kel said.

"I learned how to use some of these things by watching my father and my husband, but there are plenty I *can't* use, and I can't make *any* new ones."

"So you know how to use the...the fill-dirt-presses?" Ezak asked.

Dorna frowned. "No," she said. "That was one reason I planned to sell it. I know a few patterns, but I don't really understand how to work it properly. That's probably going to make catching it tricky."

Kel and Ezak exchanged glances. "*How* tricky?" Ezak asked.

Dorna sighed. "I wish I knew," she said.

SIX

Early that afternoon they stopped for lunch in a meadow, forty yards beyond the end of a huge wheat field, where a broken fence and a few widely-spaced trees had seemed to indicate a boundary of some sort. Ezak had been suggesting a stop, more and more pointedly every time, since mid-morning, and Dorna had gone from ignoring him to simply telling him to shut up until at last, at least an hour after the sun had passed its zenith, she had finally agreed.

They had passed several farmhouses as they traveled, and Ezak had pointed out that the farmers would probably be happy to sell them some food, but when Dorna had at last deigned to stop they were in the open meadow, without a single man-made structure anywhere in sight except a couple of fenceposts and a fallen rail. Instead of buying food from a farmer's kitchen, the sorcerer's widow pulled a half-ball of hard cheese, half a dozen hard rolls, and a small jug of beer from her shoulder-bag.

"This is all the food I brought," she said, as she distributed the rolls. "I hoped it wouldn't take this long."

"I'm sorry," Kel said.

"Why are we stopping *here*, then?" Ezak demanded. "Why didn't we buy something from a farmer?"

"Because the *fil drepessis* was still moving," Dorna said. She held up the golden boot-heel. "Now it isn't."

"That thing tells you whether it's moving?" Ezak asked. "Not just the direction?"

"Yes. And it stopped."

"Why are *we* stopping, then?" Kel asked. "Shouldn't we catch it while we can?"

"The only reason it would stop," Dorna said, "is that it's found whatever it came to repair. It'll probably need a good long time to fix it, and when it's fixed it'll either stay where it is, or head back toward the inn, or go back to Nabal's workshop—I don't know which, but if it stays we can find it, and if it does either of the others it should come right to us."

"It *could* just be broken," Ezak grumbled. "You said some of those talisman things break easily."

"Not a *fil drepessis*," Dorna said. "I mean, yes, it could be broken, but nothing with *fil* in the name is fragile."

"Why?" Kel asked.

She glared at him. "How should *I* know? I'm not a sorcerer. I just know what I've seen all my life—you can whack the *fil drepessis*, or the *fil skork*, or a *fil splayoon*, with a hammer, or kick it down the stairs, and it won't even notice, where if you breathe hard on a *lagash* it needs to be taken apart, cleaned, and rebuilt before it works again." She transferred the glare to the crumbly cheese in her hand. "I wish we had a *fil splayoon* right now; the food those things make tastes better than *this* stuff."

"So it isn't moving," Ezak said. "Can you tell where it is?"

Dorna nodded as she chewed bread and cheese. "A couple of hundred yards that way," she said, once she had swallowed. She pointed in the direction they had been walking. "We'll catch it as soon as we're done eating."

That said, she settled down cross-legged on the wild grass of the meadow, and the two men followed her example, gnawing at their meal. The cheese was dry and tasteless, and the rolls were hard chewing; Kel wished the jug of beer was larger. He looked around for water, but didn't see anything close at hand that might provide a drink; they were seated in a broad, gently-rolling expanse of knee-high grass, with a few trees visible in the distance. A warm breeze was blowing, carrying odors Kel did not recognize.

When all three had eaten their fill the rolls and every drop of beer were gone, but more than half the cheese remained; Dorna wrapped it up and returned it to her bag. She brushed crumbs from her skirt, then said, "Come on," stood, and set out across the meadow without waiting to see whether the others were following.

This gave Ezak an opportunity he had been waiting for; he leaned over and whispered in Kel's ear, "If we can get that fill-dirt-presses thing for ourselves, we'll be rich!"

"I don't think that's a good idea," Kel replied, with an uneasy glance at Dorna's back.

"Why not? What's wrong with it?"

"She'll know we took it."

"So what? We'll sell it to some sorcerer in the city, we won't try to keep it."

Kel pointed. "She has that bag full of magic. I don't want her mad at me."

"Exactly, she has all that other magic! She doesn't need the fill-dirt-presses."

"I don't think it works like that." He shook his head. "I don't want to steal her magic, Ezak. I think it's a bad idea."

"You what?" Ezak glared at him. "Then what do you think we're *doing* here?"

"We're helping her get back the thing you set loose," Kel said. "Listen, you said we were going to trick her into giving us some magic. Well, that isn't going to happen—she knows we're thieves. She may not really be a sorcerer, but she has a *lot* of magic, and I don't want to make her angry."

"Then what are we supposed to do, to get a share of her husband's magic? It's not really *hers*, after all; it was *his*."

"It's hers now. She can keep it. Let's help her get to Ethshar and then go find some other way to get money."

"But we're here, and she has all that magic!"

"She has a list of it all. She can tell if any talismans are missing."

"If she bothers to check every single item, yes, but why would she *do* that?"

"Because she *knows* we came here to steal it!"

"Are you two coming?" Dorna called, before Ezak could reply.

"Come on," Kel said, setting out after her.

A few minutes later, still in the meadow, they topped a small rise, Dorna holding her sorcerous device out. "It's just ahead," she said. "We should be able to see it." She looked up from her talisman, then cried, "Look out!" and flung herself to the ground.

Kel instantly copied her, although he had no idea why. His survival instincts had been honed on the streets of Smallgate, and he didn't need a reason. As he dove, a red flash suddenly blinded him momentarily. He blinked, and landed hard on the ground. Lying flat on his belly in the grass, Kel twisted his head as his vision cleared, and peered through the tall grass to see Dorna equally prone. Ezak was not in sight, and Kel was trying to locate him when a howl from somewhere behind him drew his attention. He pushed himself up on one elbow and peered back.

Ezak was sitting on the ground just behind the low ridge in the meadow, holding the side of his head. At first Kel thought that he was seeing an after-image of the red flash, and then realized that the red stuff trickling between Ezak's fingers and down his wrist and neck was blood. The howl was coming from Ezak.

"Shut up!" Kel hissed. "They might hear us!"

Ezak, who had been looking nowhere in particular, turned to glare at his companion. "*Who* might?" he said. "It *hurts!*"

"Whoever made that flash," Kel said. He glanced ahead, but could not see anyone or anything moving.

"Stay down," Dorna said, without moving from where she lay. "I don't think it can hurt us if we stay low."

"It?" Ezak asked. He carefully took his hand from the side of his head.

"The talisman."

"The one we're chasing? It can…it *cut off the top of my ear*?" He stared into the blood-filled palm of his hand. Kel could not see what he held, but he could see that something had cut a gouge in the side of Ezak's head, a shallow gouge that was bleeding profusely. A large hank of Ezak's hair had been sliced away and had tumbled down across his shoulder and tunic, scattering black hair in the blood, and his ear looked wrong—apparently a sliver had indeed been removed from its upper curve.

"No, not that one," Dorna said, shading her eyes with one hand as she peered out across the meadow. "The one it repaired."

"*What?*" both men said in unison.

Dorna pointed. "That thing," she said.

Ezak and Kel turned to look in the direction she indicated, and Kel started to lift his head to see over the grass.

"Stay down!" she snapped. "It won't blast you if you stay hidden in the grass."

Ezak let out a low moan, and fell forward onto his belly; from Kel's vantage point he vanished behind the rise. "What *is* it?" Ezak wailed.

"I don't know," Dorna said, "but I would guess it's Northern sorcery left over from the Great War. I saw it pointing at us right before that flash."

"I'm bleeding a lot," Ezak said. "Am I going to die?"

"I don't think so," Dorna said. "Shut up and I'll see if I can help."

Kel glanced over and saw Dorna twisting around to head back over the rise, carefully staying below the top of the grass as she crawled along. He did not follow; he didn't know much of anything about caring for wounds, and if she needed his help he was sure she would ask—or order—him. Instead he scanned the land ahead, trying to locate the Northern sorcery and make sure it wasn't coming any closer.

"What's that?" he heard Ezak ask, his voice unsteady.

"A healer," Dorna replied. "Hold still."

"I never heard of healing sorcery," Ezak protested.

"You don't know much about sorcery, then. Witchcraft is usually cheaper, but sorcery can heal, too."

Kel had never heard of sorcerous healing, either, but he *had* heard that not only could witches heal injuries, but so could warlocks and wizards and theurgists. It didn't seem very surprising that sorcerers could, too. He kept his attention focused forward.

Nothing was moving, so far as he could see, unless he counted occasional small ripples where the breeze disturbed the meadow grass. He heard insects buzzing, but could not see them. Cautiously, he lifted his head and saw the afternoon sun glinting from something almost directly ahead of him, easily a hundred yards away.

"I think I see it," he said, keeping his voice low.

"What?" Dorna replied.

"I said, I think I see it," Kel repeated, a little more loudly.

"Well, of course," Dorna said angrily. "I saw it, too. That's why I said to get down, which your big clumsy friend, who has now passed out on us, chose to ignore."

"But all I see is something shiny," Kel said quietly. "How could you tell it was dangerous?"

"Will you *speak up*? It can't possibly hear us from this far away, if it can hear at all."

"I said, how could you tell it was dangerous?" Kel shouted.

"I didn't know for sure, but when I saw it swivel toward us I thought we'd better be careful."

"It swiveled?"

"Yes."

"I didn't see that. It's not moving now."

"It's probably still pointed straight at us."

"Why isn't it coming closer?"

"I don't think it can. I think it's fixed in place. The *fil drepessis* isn't moving, and I think it would be following the Northern thing if the Northern thing was moving."

"Why?"

The silence after Kel asked that was long enough that he was beginning to worry, but at last Dorna said, "You're right. It might have just shut down where it was when it finished its job. I don't know what your idiot friend told it to do."

"Neither does he," Kel said.

"So I understand."

"What do we do now?"

The pause was not quite so long and worrisome this time. "I don't know," Dorna finally said. "We need to stop that thing and get the *fil drepessis* back, but I don't know how." More quietly, she added, "I wish Nabal were here."

"So do I," Kel said to himself, too softly for the others to hear. Then more loudly, he said, "Couldn't we go find another sorcerer to take care of it? Or a wizard, or some other magician?"

"No!" Dorna said. Then a moment later she added, "At least, I'd rather not. That's *my fil drepessis* out there. I don't want anyone else to take it. And I don't want it destroyed—it might be the last one."

"But..." Kel began. Then he stopped, uncertain what he was going to say.

"It *is* mine!" Dorna snapped. "I know I'm not a sorcerer, so I'm not supposed to have it, or most of the other talismans, but Nabal never had an apprentice, living in that miserable little village the way we did, so it's *mine. I'll* decide who I sell it to!"

"But couldn't you hire someone to smash the Northern thing and leave your feel-drapes-hiss alone?"

"I don't know. Maybe. But this is my fault, so I should take care of it."

Kel blinked, and turned, but could not see the sorcerer's widow. "Why is it your fault?" he asked.

"Because I knew you two were thieves come to steal my husband's magic, and I didn't just chase you off. I thought I could outsmart you and make you work for me, and now look! Here we are in the middle of nowhere trying to fight Northern combat sorcery, and that whole wagonload of magic is sitting there at the inn just waiting for someone else to steal it!"

"Irien's watching it."

"Irien's just an innkeeper! What does she know about it?"

"Innkeepers are usually pretty good at dealing with thieves," Kel said. "It's part of the job." Almost as soon as the words left his mouth, though, he wondered whether that was as true out in the country as it was inside the city walls.

Kel heard a loud sniff before Dorna said, "I suppose you're right," and he realized she was crying quietly.

"Couldn't we go back and get your wagon safely to Ethshar, and then come back for the feel-drapes-hiss when we have a plan for catching it?" he asked. "After all, if we can't get near it, neither can anyone else. We know where it is now."

"No," Dorna said. "No, it's too dangerous. Someone might get killed. Ezak was lucky it only took off some hair and part of his ear—if he'd gotten any closer it might have cut off his whole head. Besides, even if that thing doesn't kill anyone, someone might get to it and claim the *fil drepessis* before we get back."

Kel had to admit to himself that her first point was a good one—anyone who wandered into the area unsuspecting might get cut to pieces by that red flash, and while this meadow wasn't exactly farmed, they had seen a few signs that they weren't the first people to wander through the area—trampled grass, discarded apple cores, and the like.

What *was* that flash, anyway? Northern sorcery, yes, but how did it work?

"Dorna?" he called.

"What?"

"Do you have any idea what that Northern thing is?"

"A weapon, of course."

"But what *kind* of weapon?"

"I don't know! I'm not a sorcerer, and Northern sorcery was different, anyway."

"If it's different, then how could the feel-drapes-hiss fix it?"

"It obviously wasn't *that* different! I told you, sorcery uses the natural order of the World, and that's the same everywhere. The basic principles don't change, but how they're used..." She didn't finish the sentence.

"But if the feel-drapes-hiss is Ethsharitic, why would it want to fix Northern sorcery? How would it know how?"

"I don't know!" Dorna shouted. "I don't even know for sure that the *fil drepessis* was Ethsharitic originally; it could have been Northern, for all I know."

"Oh," Kel said.

"The Northerners used sorcery more than Ethshar did in the Great War. A lot of old sorcery is Northern."

"But..." Kel frowned and stared more intently through the grass. "But the Northerners were evil, weren't they?"

"I guess so."

"Then is it safe, using their sorcery? Isn't it evil?"

"It isn't good or evil, it's magic. It's a tool. It can be *used* for good or evil."

"The demonologists say that, too," Kel said, remembering some of the testimony the magistrate had heard at his trial. "But most people think demonology is evil."

"That's different. Demons are alive—well, I *think* they are, anyway. Sorcery isn't."

"That feel-drapes-hiss looked alive to me," Kel said.

"It isn't. It's just a spell in solid form."

"Oh."

"Demonology was originally Northern magic, too," Dorna added. "Even more than sorcery. *Both* sides used sorcery, but only the Northern Empire used demons during the war."

"But we have demonologists now," Kel said.

He could almost hear Dorna turn up an empty hand. "The demons probably can't tell our demonologists aren't Northerners. Or they don't care."

Something that had been bothering Kel suddenly fell into place. "So that thing that cut off Ezak's ear is a Northern weapon from the Great War, right?"

"I assume so, yes. This area was Northern territory sometimes during the war."

"So it's supposed to kill any Ethsharites it sees?"

"Apparently."

"So how can it tell?"

"What?"

"How can it tell we're Ethsharites?"

Dorna took several seconds to answer slowly, "I don't know."

"If we could convince it we're Northerners, it would probably let us walk right up and smash it, wouldn't it?"

"It might," Dorna admitted. "It must have... I mean, the Northerners who put it there must have had some way to get past it."

"So all we have to do is convince it we're Northerners!"

"You're right," Dorna said. "That...that should work!"

Kel felt himself puffing up with pride.

"But," Dorna said, "how do we do that?"

Kel's ego abruptly deflated again. "I don't know," he admitted. "But there must be *some* way!"

"Well, if you think of one, tell me," Dorna said.

SEVEN

Kel was still lying in the tall grass on the northeast side of the little ridge when Ezak finally woke up. Kel had been trying to think of some way to make the Northern sorcery think they were Northerners, but had not yet with come up with anything more sophisticated than circling around so that they came at it from the north, instead of the southwest. Somehow he doubted that would be enough, and Dorna had agreed that it wasn't likely to work.

"It might be worth a try if we get desperate enough, though," she had said.

So he had lain there, trying to think of something else, and hoping that Ezak, who was, after all, the clever one, would have a suggestion. When Dorna finally called, "He's awake!" Kel turned and almost sat up before he remembered where he was, and what might happen if he stuck his head above the grass. Instead he began crawling back over the rise to where the others were.

Dorna was sitting cross-legged on the grass, her head bent down, while Ezak lay flat on his back beside her, blinking up at the clouds drifting lazily overhead. She had wiped off the worst of the blood, and her healing sorcery had done its job—while his ear was still missing a piece, and his hair was cut short or gone entirely on that side of his head, the wounds were closed and partially healed, looking as if the injuries had been sustained a sixnight before, rather than merely an hour or so earlier.

"How are you feeling?" Dorna asked him.

"My ear hurts," Ezak replied.

"That's hardly surprising," Dorna answered. "Anything else?"

"My head hurts." He reached up a hand to touch his wound, and winced.

"Again, not a surprise. Do you remember what happened?"

"Something…hit me?" He gingerly fingered his shortened ear, feeling its new shape.

"Northern sorcery," Dorna told him.

"There was a red light?"

"That's right."

He blinked. "It cut the top off my ear, and cut a groove into the side of my head."

"Yes."

"How long have I been lying here? It feels…" He stroked the side of his head. "Well, it doesn't feel fresh."

"I did some healing."

"Oh, that's right. I remember that. Did you put me to sleep?"

"You fainted."

Ezak winced again, then repeated, "How long have I been lying here?"

"About an hour," Kel volunteered, startling both Dorna and Ezak.

Ezak pushed himself up on his elbows and looked at his companion. "And you two have just been sitting here, waiting for me to wake up?"

"Yes," Kel said, as Dorna said, "No."

Dorna glared at Kel, then said, "We've been doing some planning."

"But we haven't come up with much," Kel added, drawing a fresh glare from Dorna.

Ezak looked from Dorna to Kel, then back. He rolled over and sat up. "What was it that cut me?"

"Northern sorcery," Dorna said. "We don't know exactly what kind. In fact, you might be able to help with that."

"Oh? How?"

"Kel and I both ducked before that red flash, so we didn't see what it was. You were looking almost directly at it. What did you see?"

"A red flash," Ezak said, as if addressing an idiot. Kel winced.

"I know that," Dorna replied. "But what *kind* of a flash? Was it a flash of light, or a burst of flame? Was it in a beam, or all over? Why did it take off your hair and trim your ear, but not cut off your entire head? Was it a fireball, or lightning, or something else?"

"Oh," Ezak said. His expression turned thoughtful. "I'm not sure," he admitted.

"Was he burned? When you healed him?" Kel asked.

"No," Dorna said.

"Then it probably wasn't a fireball, or lightning."

Dorna turned to look at him. "I thought Ezak was supposed to be the clever one."

"He is," Kel said, confused.

"It was a clean cut," Dorna said. "As if something very sharp had sliced through."

"Like...like a magical knife?" Ezak asked.

"Yes." She frowned. "So we have some idea what we're dealing with. Did you *see* a knife, Ezak?"

He shook his head. "Just a red light."

"Did you feel anything?"

"Of course I did!" Ezak said. "I felt pain!"

"Yes, but what *kind* of pain? Did it feel like a knife was cutting you?"

"I..." Ezak stopped to think, then said, "I didn't feel anything happen—one second I was fine, and the next I was bleeding all over and my ear and head hurt like death."

"So it's very, very fast, whatever it is. It probably didn't just throw an ordinary knife. More likely it was raw magic."

Ezak asked the question Kel was thinking—"So what? What difference does it make?"

"So I'm trying to think whether it might run out of ammunition, or whether we might be able to make shields or armor that would protect us while we get close to it."

"Oh," Ezak said, and Kel had to admit she had a good reason for her questions.

"Kel and I were thinking it must be Northern military sorcery, so if we can convince it we're Northerners it won't hurt us, but we don't know how to do that, so I was thinking about shields, or making it use up whatever it's throwing at us. Except if it's throwing pure *gaja* at us, it can't run out, ever—the World is *full* of *gaja*."

"It is?" Ezak asked, startled.

"Yes. It is. Or sorcery would have stopped working a long time ago, when the *gaja* was used up."

"Oh." Ezak considered this. "So...the top of my ear was cut off by some left-over Northern sorcery that's throwing knives made of pure magical energy at us?"

Dorna nodded. "So it would seem," she said.

"It throws them at anyone it sees?"

"Apparently."

"But you don't think it would throw them at Northerners?"

"Right. The magician who made it wouldn't want to hurt his own people."

"How did it know we *aren't* Northerners? I mean, they weren't demons, were they? They were people, like us."

Dorna opened her mouth to answer, then closed it again. She looked to the northeast and frowned, then looked back at Ezak. "You know, every time I think you two are both idiots, you surprise me by saying something smart. Why *did* it assume we're enemies?"

"It probably thinks *everyone* is," Kel said. "Maybe it knows there aren't any more Northerners."

"This thing that cut off my ear," Ezak said. "What *is* it? How smart is it? I thought we were talking about a talisman, a spell, but you're talking about it as if it's a person, or a creature."

"We don't know what it is," Dorna said. "Or how smart it is. But some talismans are...well, they can do things. They can talk. They can see. They can hear. You saw the *fil drepessis*—is that a spell or a creature?"

Ezak considered that for a moment, then said, "I see your point."

"Whatever it is, there was *something* here that made it think it should attack us," Kel said.

"So it would seem," Dorna said.

Kel looked at her, trying to guess what might have made the Northern sorcery think she was an Ethsharite. She was wearing a dark green dress, with her long black hair pulled back and loosely bound in a soft green ribbon, and she had that canvas bag over her shoulder.

Ezak was wearing a tan cotton tunic that had seen better days, and brown leather breeches. His curly hair—what remained of it—was a little longer than was fashionable, but reasonably tidy.

Kel himself was wearing a dark red tunic and gray goatskin breeches, and his hair just covered his ears. They all looked ordinary enough. Had Northerners looked different, back when Northerners still existed?

A memory came to him. Ethshar's city guards wore red and yellow now, but during the war they hadn't. Kel thought back to pictures he had seen of soldiers in the Great War—there were murals on the walls of the magistrate's hall back in Smallgate, and he had seen a tapestry in the south tower in Grandgate once. In those pictures, the Ethsharitic soldiers wore green and brown, while the Northerners—well, the Northerners were mostly indistinct figures in the distance, but they appeared to be wearing black and gray.

Dorna was wearing green. Ezak was wearing brown. But Kel himself was wearing red and gray, and during the war those weren't the colors for either side. After the war the overlords dressed their soldiers in red and yellow, but it was a completely different shade of red, much brighter than the drab hue of Kel's tunic, and anyway, how would a leftover spell from the Great War know about the change?

"Wait here," he said.

"What?" Dorna turned to look at him, but Kel was already on his feet and running southeast, behind the low ridge.

"What are you *doing*?" the sorcerer's widow shouted after him.

"Trying something," Kel called back.

"Trying *what*?"

Kel was not sure just how to explain his idea, so he didn't answer that. He got a hundred yards away from the others—he thought that should be far enough—then got down on hands and knees, and crawled up over the rise, staying hidden in the tall grass.

Then once he was over the rise, he stood up, prepared to drop to his belly if he saw a red flash. He scanned the area where he judged the Northern talisman to be, and caught the glint of sunlight on metal. He could see something shaped sort of like a horn, but with less of a flared opening than usual, atop a dark cylinder sticking up out of the grass; it swiveled toward him, and he tensed, getting ready to dive for safety.

Then it stopped, and swiveled back until it was once again aimed at Dorna and Ezak.

Maybe it didn't think he was a Northerner, but it didn't think he was a threat, either. It was ignoring him.

"*Hai*!" he called, waving at it.

The horn-shaped thing swung toward him again, then seemed to hesitate. It shifted a little further, then turned back toward the others.

In the distance he heard Dorna shouting at him, "What are you *doing*, you lunatic?"

He smiled, and began walking across the meadow toward the Northern talisman. If he was right, he told himself, if it really thought he was a Northerner, he ought to be able to walk right up to it and retrieve the…the *fil* whatever-it-is.

"Kel!" Dorna shrieked. "Get down!"

He turned, and could see her lying on the ground, peeping through the grass at him. He waved to her, then kept walking.

He was perhaps sixty feet from the Northern sorcery, whatever it was, when the horn suddenly swung toward him again, and a loud, masculine, unfamiliar voice said something in a foreign language, a language he didn't recognize.

Kel stopped walking. He didn't know what the voice had said, but it had the sound of a warning. The thing hadn't given any warning before slicing Ezak's ear off, but it had apparently thought Ezak was an enemy, where it appeared to accept Kel as a friend, or at least neutral.

Cautiously, Kel took a step backward. The horn thing seemed to hesitate. He backed up another step, and it swung around to point back toward Dorna and Ezak.

So it would let him get close, but not *too* close. It didn't attack him just because it could, but it didn't let him walk right up to it, either. That seemed sensible enough. He smiled, turned, and headed directly toward the others.

"What did you do?" Dorna called, as he drew near enough for conversation. "How did you do that? How did you know?"

"I didn't *know*," Kel replied. "I guessed. I was ready to duck if it pointed at me, but it didn't."

"Why *not*?" she demanded. "We couldn't really see from down here—what did you do?"

"Nothing," Kel said. "It wasn't attacking *me* in the first place. All I had to do was get away from you two."

Dorna considered this for a moment as Kel continued to march toward her through the tall grass, then asked, "Why?"

"Because you're wearing green," Kel said proudly. He had figured this out all by himself. "And Ezak is wearing brown."

Dorna stared at him. "What difference does *that* make?"

"Well, you said it was left from the Great War, and in the Great War Ethshar's soldiers wore green and brown, while the Northerners wore black and gray."

"They did?"

"Yes."

"*I* didn't know that. How did *you* know that?"

"From pictures back in Ethshar. In the magistrate's hall in Smallgate."

"Well, I'll be a toad. You really think that's it?"

Kel nodded vigorously. "What else could it be? We were trying to guess how it could tell Northerners from Ethsharites; well, how did the soldiers in the Great War tell them apart? From the colors of their uniforms. Why shouldn't this talisman be doing the same thing?"

"Every time I think you two are hopelessly stupid..." Dorna sighed. "All right. But you turned back before you got right up to it, and I thought I heard something—what happened?"

"It pointed at me and said something," Kel explained. "It sounded like a warning, but I don't know the language it spoke, so I'm not sure. I thought it didn't want to let me get *too* close—probably because I'm not in a Northern uniform."

"I suppose civilians generally wouldn't be allowed near it," Dorna agreed. "So you think if we were wearing black and gray we could walk right up to it?"

Kel turned up an empty palm. "Maybe. I don't know whether it wants just the right colors, or the actual uniforms."

"Good point. We probably can't fake the uniforms—we might have the wrong length tunic, or something." Kel had almost reached the ridge now, and could see Dorna's face where she crouched behind it; she looked very thoughtful. Ezak, sitting behind her, looked bored.

Kel ambled up over the rise, then sat down in the grass beside Dorna. Their actions had trampled out an area perhaps a dozen feet across, and Kel found a smooth spot to sit near one side of this cleared patch.

"If I can get close enough, I can blast it," Dorna said, reaching for her canvas bag. "I brought a couple of weapons.

They can't hit it from here, but if I can get close enough..."
She frowned. "How close were you when it warned you off?"

Kel was good at estimating distances; it was a useful skill
for a thief to have when climbing around rooftops or up and
down walls. "At least fifty feet," he said. "But less than sixty-
five."

"That should be close enough," Dorna said, digging
through the bag. Things clattered and clanked as she searched,
but then she pulled out something black and about the size
and shape of a hound's foreleg.

Kel hesitated. "Do you want me to use that?" he asked.
"I'm not good with magic."

Dorna looked up, startled. "You? Gods and stars, no. I
wouldn't trust you with this thing even if I thought you *could*
learn to use it. I'll do it."

"But...you're wearing green."

She looked down at herself. "Yes, I know," she said. "I'll
have to take off my dress."

"But..." Kel could not complete his protest.

"You don't need to blush. I'm wearing a shift under it. A
white one, which should be safe."

"Oh," Kel said, relieved.

Dorna stood up, untied her belt, and began tugging at her
skirt. Kel quickly turned away, looking out over the meadow
toward the Northern talisman.

A moment later Dorna said, "There!" Kel turned back to
see her standing there in her shift.

Never having seen a woman clad only in her undergar-
ments before he had not been sure just what to expect, but
even so, he was startled. The shift was a simple sleeve-
less white garment supported by two straps over Dorna's
shoulders; it exposed far more of her breasts than Kel had

expected, and ended just above her knee, reminding Kel of a little girl's summer tunic and making her look far younger than her years. She had removed her green ribbon and let her hair down, which added to the youthful effect.

The shift was almost transparent; Kel had never seen so revealing a fabric. The cheapest whore in Soldiertown was generally not as exposed as this. Despite what Dorna had said, Kel did blush.

Ezak whistled, and Dorna turned around to slap him, deliberately aiming for his injured ear. He ducked, but the blow still brushed across his head just above his half-healed wound, and Ezak winced.

"Well," Dorna said, "Let's see if this works." She reached down and lifted the canvas bag onto her shoulder, then took the black weapon in hand and stepped forward, up the little ridge.

There was a red flash.

EIGHT

Dorna dropped to the ground; an instant later, so did Kel.

He had been standing with his back to the Northern device, so he had had no warning, and had not ducked until he saw the flash, but then he had flung himself down vigorously enough that a blade of grass had gone up his nose, and he could smell the dirt beneath. He snorted out the grass and pushed himself up enough to free his hands, then quickly patted first his head and then his shoulders to see if he felt blood anywhere. He seemed unhurt.

"Are you all right?" he called, staying low.

Dorna's response included suggestions that made Kel blush even more than her undressed state had; he was fairly sure at least one was physically impossible. When she had calmed down a little, she shouted, "Apparently it wasn't the green dress."

"I guess not," Kel replied miserably. "Are you hurt?"

"No. My hair's shorter on one side, though."

Kel lifted his head further and peered through the grass, but he could not see the others—the contour of the land hid them both. With a glance over his shoulder in the direction of the Northern talisman, he got slowly to his feet, ready to drop again at the first hint of another red flash.

No flash came. He stood, and stared out over the meadow.

The talisman was still there, and the horn-thing was pointed at him—or at Dorna, or Ezak; they were close enough together it could have been any of them.

He turned around to see Dorna struggling to pull her dress back on while staying below the thing's line of sight. As her head emerged from the collar he could see that the red flash had indeed cut away a hank of hair on the left side.

It had cut the top off Ezak's *right* ear. Why would it be different? Why would it strike to one side at all, instead of right down the middle? It shouldn't just be poor aim; this wasn't a person, it was *magic*.

Maybe it wasn't aiming for her head at all. Maybe, Kel thought, it hadn't been aiming at *Ezak* at all. Ezak had been *behind* Dorna. And it obviously hadn't been aiming at *him*—he was standing right here in plain sight, and it wasn't throwing anything at him.

It hadn't been aiming for the green dress, either, but Kel thought back to what he had seen a moment before. Dorna had been standing there in her shift, with her sorcerous weapon in her right hand, and the canvas bag slung on her left shoulder…

The magical blade had struck her on her left, as she dropped. Her head must have already been halfway to the ground when her long hair was chopped off.

"It was aiming at the bag," Kel said, pointing.

"What?" Dorna looked up from tying her belt.

"It hit the hair on the left as you went down," Kel said. "It was aiming for the bag."

She looked down at the bag where it lay on the trampled grass to her left, then at a hank of black hair that lay beside the bag. "Blood and death," she said. "You're right."

"Why would it do that?" Ezak asked. He was still sitting just where he had been all along; he had not stood up when Dorna did.

"Sorcery," Dorna said. "It must sense the sorcery in the bag."

"But it *is* sorcery!" Ezak said.

"It must be able to tell that some of what I have here is Ethsharitic," Dorna said.

"Is your weapon Ethsharitic?" Kel asked, pointing.

Dorna picked up the black thing and looked at it. "I don't know," she said. "I never thought it mattered."

"It didn't try to hit *that*."

Dorna glanced at Kel, then looked at the weapon again.

"The bag was a bigger target," Ezak said.

"That's true," Dorna said, still studying the weapon. Then she looked around. The sun was moving down the western sky; they had spent most of the day pursuing the *fil drepessis* or dodging the Northern device's attacks. She tucked the weapon in her belt, then swung around and began moving behind the ridge, sometimes on hands and knees, sometimes on her feet but bent almost double.

When she was about fifty feet away from the canvas bag she took a deep breath, then straightened up and looked out across the ridge and the meadow. Kel turned, too.

The Northern talisman was not moving. The horn, or tube, or whatever it was was still pointed toward the ridge in front of the trampled area where Ezak sat and the canvas bag lay.

"It's not throwing anything at me," Dorna said.

Kel nodded, though he realized that Dorna was not looking at him and probably did not see the gesture. He turned to watch her.

She raised the weapon, her gaze fixed intently on the Northern device. She waved it back and forth; the talisman did not react. "Whatever it doesn't like must be in the bag," she said.

No one answered. Kel glanced at Ezak; he was crouching behind the ridge, watching Dorna.

The sorcerer's widow took a cautious step forward, then another.

No reaction.

She began walking slowly forward.

She had gone perhaps fifty feet, Kel watching every step, when he was distracted by a hissing. He turned to see Ezak beckoning to him.

He gave Dorna one more quick glance, then hurried up over the rise to where Ezak sat. "What is it?" he asked.

"Here's our chance," Ezak said. "We can take the bag and run!"

Kel blinked at him.

"She won't even notice!" Ezak said. "She's too busy with that thing over there." He waved in the direction of the Northern talisman.

Kel shook his head.

"Why not? She's probably going to get herself killed! Even if she doesn't, we can get a good head start—we don't need to go back for the wagon, there's probably enough here to make us rich. We can just pick a direction, and she'll never be able to find us without her magic."

"No," Kel said.

"Why *not*? What's wrong with you? Here's our chance!"

"No," Kel repeated, shaking his head again for emphasis.

"What is it? You think she'll find us somehow?"

In fact, now that Ezak mentioned it, Kel *did* think it was likely that she would come after them, and she had far more sorcery back in the wagon than was here in her shoulder-bag, so she would probably be able to find them. Even if she couldn't do it with her inherited talismans, she could always hire a wizard or a theurgist to locate the stolen goods. And she had *said* that if he stole from her, she would track Ezak down and kill him.

That was not why Kel had said no, though. That had not even occurred to him until Ezak brought it up. His objection was far more simple, and far more basic.

Taking that bag of magic now would be wrong.

Kel did not think *all* theft was wrong; he could not have survived on the streets of Smallgate if he had taken so absolute a position. He was perfectly willing to steal from those who could afford it, or those who deserved it. He had never objected to robbing other thieves, or cutting the purse off a rich man's belt. He was perfectly willing to steal a few coins from the bar at the Bent Sword because everyone knew that Dulbek, the proprietor, watered the beer and shortchanged anyone drunk enough that Dulbek thought they might not notice a missing bit or two. Grabbing money from a dice game was just fine, since the players had put it at risk in the first place.

But Dorna was out there trying to protect people by removing that Northern sorcery. She was risking her life. She had done nothing to Kel or Ezak to deserve betrayal. Yes, she had tricked them into helping her move her belongings, but they had been trying to rob her; that sort of turnabout was only fair.

She could have sent one of them out to blast that thing. She knew Kel could get close to it. But she hadn't; she was going out there herself. If that talisman belatedly noticed the weapon in her hand when she got close, she wouldn't have time to dodge the next magical blade.

"If it kills her," he said, "*then* we can take it."

"What? Why can't we take it now?"

"It isn't fair."

"*Life* isn't fair, Kel! You know that better than anyone!"

"Well, we should try to be better than that."

"Fine!" Ezak threw up his hands. "Fine! We'll wait until it kills her. She probably *would* track us down, anyway." He folded his hands across his chest and sat glowering at the canvas bag.

Kel watched him for a moment, then turned and walked back up the rise to see how Dorna was doing.

She was moving cautiously across the meadow, the weapon in her hand, eyes fixed on the Northern talisman. She was about halfway. She looked very small out there in the broad open space, and it occurred to Kel that she would probably need help carrying the *fil drepessis* back after she got it away from the device it had fixed. She had said she didn't really know how to use it properly, so she probably couldn't just tell it to walk back to the inn. If she had some magical transport in mind, that would presumably be in with her other sorcery; she would still need to get the talisman back to where she had left the bag.

"I'm going to help her," Kel said. Then he started trotting across the meadow.

"Have fun," Ezak called after him.

Kel did not bother to answer.

Dorna was about sixty feet from the Northern device, and Kel was perhaps two-thirds of the way across the meadow, when that loud voice spoke again, saying exactly the same thing it had said when *he* was about twenty yards away. Dorna stopped dead.

"Do you know what it said?" Kel called.

Dorna turned, startled, and Kel realized she hadn't noticed him following her until now. "No," she answered. "I don't. It sounds vaguely familiar, though. I think it might be asking for a password."

"Do you know a password?"

"No," Dorna said, as she raised the weapon and pointed it at the talisman.

The vaguely tube-shaped structure on the top of the device pivoted toward her, and Kel shouted, "Look out!"

Dorna dropped her weapon and raised her empty hands. Kel guessed that she did not think she could drop out of its target area quickly enough at this distance.

"Apparently it defends itself," Dorna said, standing very still.

Kel agreed. The device must have seen the weapon before, and recognized that it was a weapon, but it was only when Dorna pointed it at the talisman that it reacted. He did not say anything, but hurried through the tall grass toward her. A moment later he stood beside her, then stooped down to retrieve the fallen weapon. Holding it loosely, not pointing it anywhere, he looked from Dorna to the talisman.

It stood perhaps three or four feet tall, a dark gray cylinder with that shiny hornlike thing on top. It had no other visible features, and Kel could not detect any sound or odor from it. He could see beside it, half-hidden by the tall grass, the *fil drepessis*.

The Northern device spoke again, the same phrase as before. The horn stayed pointed at Dorna.

Kel sidled away from her, to see whether the thing would follow him, now that he had the weapon. It did not; apparently it had decided that Dorna was more likely to be an enemy, despite her immediate surrender.

"Do you think it understands Ethsharitic?" Kel asked.

"Probably not," Dorna said. "It may not understand anything except the password."

Kel nodded, then turned to the talisman. "*Hai!*" he called. "Can you tell us where we are? We're lost."

It did not respond.

He took a step toward it, and the tube immediately swung toward him as it said something incomprehensible. He stepped back.

"If it can't understand us," he said, "then we can make a plan and it won't know what we're saying."

"Maybe," Dorna said. She did not sound entirely convinced, but she lowered her hands.

"Are we close enough for your weapon to kill it?" Kel watched the Northern device closely; it did not react, so far as he could see.

"It's not alive."

"You know what I mean."

"If we could get a clear shot at it, yes, I think so. But it's faster than a human being; if you point the weapon at it, it'll kill you before you can shoot."

"I was thinking maybe I could distract it while you shoot it."

"Well, right now *you* have the weapon, I don't!"

"I'm going to pass it to you behind my back. Then I'm going to move around, and get it to point that top piece at me. Then you can shoot it before it can swing back."

"Maybe," Dorna said again, sounding even less convinced.

"Maybe if you get down in the grass, and shoot it from there?"

"Maybe," Dorna said again. "I don't know how far it can lower its aim."

"It didn't kill us when we were on the ground over there," Kel said, pointing back toward the rise where he had left Ezak.

Dorna did not answer that. Instead she turned to look at Kel. "Since when are you clever enough to be making these plans?"

Kel blinked, and turned to stare at her. "I'm not clever," he said.

"You seem pretty clever to *me*, right now," she replied.

He shook his head. "No, I'm just making stuff up. You need to tell me which parts aren't stupid."

"So far as I can tell, *none* of it is stupid," she said. "It may not work, but it's not stupid."

Kel found that confusing—if it wouldn't work, how could it *not* be stupid? He said nothing.

"I thought Ezak was supposed to be the smart one," Dorna added.

"He is," Kel said. "He's older than me. He's always been smarter. He's always kept me safe and told me what to do."

"Why isn't he here now?"

That question baffled Kel. "He…he doesn't want to be," he said at last. "He's wounded."

"He's *scared*, if you ask me."

"Ezak isn't afraid of anything!" Kel protested.

"Yes, he is," Dorna said.

Kel decided he didn't want to talk about Ezak any more. He walked casually along what he judged to be the edge of the area where the Northern device would threaten them, looping back toward Dorna. He tried to think like Ezak, to say what Ezak would say if this were one of his schemes they were carrying out.

The horn-piece did not move; it remained pointed at the spot where he had approached too closely. Apparently it considered them both harmless for the moment.

"Look at the talisman," Kel said, as he approached Dorna, "and have your hands ready."

Dorna did as he said, and as he walked behind her he shoved the weapon into her waiting hand.

The Northern device did not move. Kel walked past Dorna, circling further around the talisman. He eyed it as he moved, wondering whether it might be able to throw magic out both ends of the horn at once. They weren't the same shape, but both did appear to have openings.

"Tell me when you're ready," he called to Dorna. He glanced over.

She had knelt down, keeping the weapon out of sight behind her back. Now, as he watched, she lowered herself down on all fours, then flat on her belly, the weapon hidden in the folds of her skirt—her *green* skirt, which the talisman had not mistaken for an Ethsharitic uniform after all. Kel was embarrassed at the memory of his foolish notion. He wondered why Ezak hadn't told him it was a stupid idea. Maybe Ezak had just wanted to see Dorna with her dress off.

She rolled over on her side for a moment, adjusting the weapon's position—or at least, that's what Kel thought she was doing. He couldn't actually see much through the tall grass.

"Ready," she called.

Kel nodded, and took a deep breath, and stepped toward the Northern talisman. "*Hai!*" he called. "I think I'll just come kick you, you know that? Here I come!" He started to run.

That strange deep voice spoke its warning, and the gleaming horn-piece pivoted toward him. He flung himself at the ground, wrapping his arms over his head—flung himself *forward*, closer to the Northern talisman, so that it would not turn its attention back to Dorna. He expected at any instant to see that deadly red flash.

Instead he saw a *blue* flash, and then the whole World seemed to vanish in a blinding white light. An overwhelming, painfully loud roar of thunder left his ears ringing, and the earth seemed to shake beneath him as he landed upon it. He wondered whether this was what dying was like as everything went dark and silent.

But he could still feel the crisp grass beneath his outthrust arms and hands, and he could smell something burning, and he realized his eyes were closed. He opened them, and lifted his head.

The top half of the Northern device was gone, and the stump of the gray cylinder was a smoking ruin, where the torn metal edges were glowing red-hot.

He still couldn't hear anything, though—but his ears were still ringing, and he realized that the explosion had deafened him temporarily. He sat up and looked around.

Dorna was sitting in the grass forty feet away, on the other side of the destroyed Northern talisman; her hair had been blown back from her face, which was streaked with smoke. She was staring in comic astonishment at the sorcerous weapon in her hand.

"Are you all right?" he called, but he could barely hear his own words.

Dorna looked up at him, then back at the weapon. Then she started shaking; her mouth came open, and her eyes closed, and at first Kel thought she was hurt, or at least frightened.

Then he realized she was laughing.

NINE

It took another several seconds before Kel's hearing finally came back, and before he and Dorna were able to confirm that they were both unhurt.

"That was *loud*," Kel said, looking around at the scattered shards of metal. At least a dozen patches of grass were scorched where hot fragments had landed, though none seemed to be actually burning; that was presumably the source of the smell he had noticed immediately after the explosion.

"They probably heard it in Sardiron," Dorna agreed.

"Did you know it would be that loud?"

She shook her head, then raised the hand holding her weapon. "I never used this thing before. I'm not sure whether most of that was from *my* magic, or from the Northern talisman." She got to her feet and tucked the weapon in her belt.

Kel started to get up, too, but stopped when he heard Dorna's sharp intake of breath. "What is it?" he said, looking up. "Isn't it…"

"The *fil drepessis*," Dorna replied. "It's trying to fix it."

"What?" Kel straightened up and looked.

Sure enough, the *fil drepessis* was moving again, and was using its dozen clawed legs to collect the scattered bits of the Northern device. It was moving with astonishing speed.

"We need to stop it," Dorna said.

Kel looked at her expectantly.

"I'm not sure I know how," she said. "I mean, I know some things about it, but I don't know what Ezak did to it. He might have changed something." She looked back toward where they had taken shelter earlier, and shouted, "Ezak! Come here!"

There was no response. A horrible thought struck Kel.

"Ezak!"

There was still no answer. "Maybe he's asleep," Kel suggested.

"After *that*?" Dorna said, pointing at the smoldering wreckage. "More likely he's still deaf."

"Maybe," Kel said unhappily. He was not about to say so, but he thought it was far more likely that Ezak wasn't there at all. He had probably run off with that bag of talismans the moment Kel was out of sight over the ridge.

Dorna frowned, and Kel thought she was considering going to fetch Ezak to help them. "He doesn't know what he did," Kel said. "He was just slapping it wildly."

"You're probably right," Dorna admitted, turning her attention back to the *fil drepessis* and the ruined Northern device. "So how do we make it stop fixing that thing?"

Kel looked. It was still gathering fragments, and he remembered what Dorna had told them about talismans being made of exactly the right metals and crystals. It could *repair* things, it couldn't *make* them.

So it needed all the pieces.

It was easier to act than to explain; he dashed forward and snatched up a shiny chunk of gray metal, the biggest one he saw, not counting the base of the cylinder. He almost dropped it again; it was *hot*. Instead he juggled it from hand to hand until he was able to wrap it in the hem of his tunic, which served to insulate it enough that he could hang onto it, though he could smell cloth scorching. This was his best tunic—really, his *only* intact tunic—and he knew this was going to ruin it, but he didn't see any other choice. Once he had the piece secured, he turned around and ran.

The *fil drepessis* paused, screamed as it had back in the wagon, then came after him, still screaming, moving in that bizarre multi-legged trot it had used when it first left the stableyard.

"Wait!" Dorna shouted, as she followed them.

Kel did not wait; he dashed across the meadow.

When he topped the rise, he saw exactly what he had feared—Ezak was gone. The canvas bag of sorcery was gone. *Everything* was gone—Ezak must have systematically collected every last item they had brought with them, from Dorna's talismans to the bloody cloth used to clean his wounds. Nothing remained but a circle of trampled grass.

He glanced back. The *fil drepessis* was still pursuing him, scarcely a dozen feet away. He had slowed to survey their huddling place; now he picked up his pace again.

"Wait!" Dorna called again, from somewhere behind him. He could barely hear her over the talisman's shrieking.

Kel did not wait. He had done this sort of thing before, though previously his pursuers had always been human—usually merchants or guardsmen. He knew not to pause, even briefly. Keep moving, that was the rule. Dodge when possible, take unexpected directions, go places the people chasing him couldn't reach or wouldn't fit, but most of all, *keep moving*.

The screaming made it hard to think. Ordinarily he had a destination in mind—usually wherever he and Ezak were living, whether it was an alley, or a cellar, or the attic above Uncle Vezalis' place on Archer Street, or even the Wall Street

Field. The first priority, though, was to lose the pursuit, and *then* worry about getting home.

Losing the *fil drepessis* was likely to be difficult, especially out here in open country where there were no corners to dodge around, no carts to hide behind, no walls to climb, no crowds to blend into. It probably didn't have the usual human limitations— he suspected it wouldn't need to sleep, and it wouldn't tire, and it couldn't be distracted or fooled by any of his usual tricks. He couldn't hope to just outrun it and go back home to Ethshar of the Sands.

So he needed another destination, one closer at hand. He had originally hoped Ezak was still there, and could slap at the glowing squares on the thing's top as it went past, but Ezak was gone.

He might be able to stay ahead of the thing all the way back to the Golden Rooster, in Shepherd's Well, but he doubted it. He had not slept since about midnight, and had eaten only one small meal in that time; he was already tired.

He didn't remember any useful landmarks along the route; they had cut through farms and meadows, and they had all looked much alike to Kel's city-bred eyes. He didn't know where Ezak had gone, and didn't see an obvious trail.

But that left one other possibility. He was not going to wait for Dorna, but he decided he was going to loop back to her and see if *she* could stop the *fil drepessis* somehow.

He slowed to let the *fil drepessis* get closer, then suddenly dodged sideways, turned left, and put on a fresh burst of speed, running behind the ridge. The *fil drepessis* turned to follow him, still screaming; a glance back over his shoulder showed him that it had made the turn more efficiently than he had hoped. He turned left again, charging up and over the ridge, and out across the meadow.

Dorna was standing in the middle of the meadow, off to his left, holding her ears; he made a third turn and headed straight for her, calling, "Can you stop it?"

"I don't..." she began.

Then he was skidding to a stop beside her, holding the fragment of Northern sorcery over his head.

"Try," he said, as the *fil drepessis* came rushing toward them.

The talisman did not hesitate; still screaming, it began to run right up Kel's body, those strange black claws grabbing at his clothes, metal legs wrapping around him.

Dorna grabbed for it, then caught herself and waited until the thing was standing on Kel's shoulders, stretching three claws up toward the fragment, leaving the glowing blue squares facing her. She reached out and tapped a sequence.

Kel could not see clearly just what had happened, since two metal legs were across his face and the main body of the *fil drepessis* was on his right shoulder, but the screaming abruptly stopped, and he glimpsed a change in color—blue reflecting on one of the metal legs suddenly mixed with yellow. The talisman stopped moving, and said something in that strange language. Dorna tapped again, in an almost musical rhythm.

It said a single two-syllable word that sounded almost like "coffer," then climbed back off him, settled to the ground, and folded itself up into its original compact form, the legs sliding into slots in the side of the main body and becoming ribs again. A heap of fragments of the ruined Northern device spilled out of it and lay on the grass beside it.

For a moment Kel and Dorna both simply stood there, panting and looking down at the *fil drepessis*.

"I wasn't sure that would work," Dorna said.

"I'm glad it did," Kel said. "What did you do?"

"Something Nabal taught me," she said. "It's a pattern—you tap it out to the tune of 'Harbor Bells,' and it shuts down the *fil drepessis*. It works on several other talismans, too."

"'Harbor Bells'?" That was one of the few songs Kel actually knew, though he always forgot the words to the second verse. "I didn't hear any music."

"I was…it was in my head," Dorna said. "I didn't need to sing it out loud, so long as I tapped the buttons that went with the tune."

"Oh." Kel glanced around, then pointed. "Are we going to do anything about the Northern talisman?"

Dorna shook her head. "It's broken," she said. "It isn't going to hurt anyone. Besides, it was dug into the ground, and I don't know how far down it goes. I wouldn't know how to get it out, and what would I do with it if I did? I don't know how to control it. It's been there for a couple of hundred years; as far as I'm concerned, it can stay for a couple of hundred more."

"Oh," Kel said.

They stood a moment longer, considering the *fil drepessis*; then Dorna looked up. "Where's Ezak? I think he should be the one to carry it back."

"Oh," Kel said again. "Um. He's gone."

Dorna turned to stare at him. "Gone? What do you mean, gone?"

"He's gone," Kel said miserably. "He ran off with your bag."

"He *what*?" She turned and stormed over to the top of the ridge, where she looked down at the empty space where Ezak should have been.

Kel stayed in the meadow, watching and chewing his lower lip. Only when Dorna had turned and was marching back, fists clenched and brows lowered in fury, did it occur to him that he could run away himself. Dorna wasn't much taller than he was, and she was probably at least twenty years older, and he had far more experience at such things; he could almost certainly get away from *her*, unlike the *fil drepessis*, and then head for Ethshar. He could find Ezak—if he wasn't in their usual hiding places, he could be reached through his Uncle Vezalis. If Ezak wasn't back in his uncle's attic, he would almost certainly have left word there. Vezalis had never liked Kel, nor Ezak, for that matter, but family was family; he would give Kel any message Ezak told him to give. Especially if Ezak had promised him a share of the proceeds from selling the stolen magic.

But that would be…well, Kel wasn't sure what it would be, but he wasn't going to do it. He was going to help Dorna get the *fil drepessis* safely back to Shepherd's Well. After that, there would be plenty of time to go back to Smallgate and find Ezak.

He stooped and picked up the *fil drepessis*. It was heavy, as he had expected, but not unmanageable. With an effort, he heaved it up onto his shoulder.

"Ezak, you stinking son of a minor demon, get *back* here!" Dorna shouted, waving her fist in the air. Kel shook his head. That wouldn't do any good; Ezak did what he pleased, regardless of what anyone said. He always had, and Kel supposed he always would. When they were children Kel had admired Ezak for it, but more recently he had begun to wish Ezak would behave better; he was tired of running and hiding and having no other friends. Kel began trudging toward the sorcerer's widow, the heavy talisman on his shoulder.

He was about twenty feet away when Dorna turned and saw him. "I suppose *you're* going to steal *that*, now?" she said.

"No," Kel said, not stopping. The possibility had not even occurred to him. "I'm just taking my turn carrying it. It's a long way back to Shepherd's Well, so I thought we might as well get started."

Dorna glared at him as he approached. "I can't stop you from taking it," she said. "I don't have any more magic."

"You have that crooked black weapon. Or you could just trip me, or hit me with something—I can't run or dodge while I'm carrying this, it's too heavy. But I'm not stealing it."

"Why *not*?"

Kel sighed. "Because you have the weapon and I can't run, and because I don't want to. It's yours."

Dorna stared at him for another few seconds, then burst into tears.

Kel stopped. He considered putting down the *fil drepessis* to comfort her, but the thought of lifting it again once it was off his shoulder was daunting, and he didn't really understand why she was upset, and he had no right to touch her. Instead, after a brief pause, he resumed his slow walk and said, "Come on. Irien is waiting."

She was still snuffling as he trudged past her, but she turned and followed him.

They had gone most of a mile, and Dorna had dried her eyes, when she said, "I suppose you're going to meet Ezak somewhere and split the loot."

Kel needed one hand to steady the talisman, but he turned up the other one. "We don't have anything planned," he said. "But I can probably find him back in Ethshar, and he'll probably give me a share, if there's anything to share."

"What do you mean, if there's anything to share? The sorcery in that bag must be worth fifty rounds of gold!"

"Is it *really*?" Kel asked, astonished. "That's a lot of money." It was, in fact, an almost unimaginable amount of money.

"The thing on your shoulder is worth at least twice that," Dorna replied.

Kel glanced at the talisman on his shoulder. It was large and heavy, but it was compact, and the leg-ribs made it easy to hold onto. It did not look as if it was worth all that money, but he knew he wasn't a very good judge of value, so he didn't say anything..

"Why wouldn't there be anything to share?" Dorna demanded.

Kel sighed. "Because," he said, "when Ezak gets it back to Ethshar he'll either take it to one of the fences in Smallgate, the people who buy and sell stolen things—"

"I know what a fence is," Dorna interrupted.

"Oh. Well, he'll either take it to a fence, or he'll go to Wizard Street in Eastside and look for a buyer there. The thing is, most of the fences don't like him and don't trust him. He's broken a lot of promises, and sold them things that weren't what he said they were. They might just take the bag from him, beat him up, and throw him in a gutter somewhere; it's not as if a thief can go to the magistrate about someone stealing the things he stole."

"Oh," Dorna said.

"Or he might try to hide most of the magic, and sell it a little at a time, so the buyer would pay up to get the rest, but that doesn't always work. When Perrea the Rat-Chaser tried that with the stuff she stole from the ruins when Firizal the Blue accidentally turned himself into a dragon and wrecked his shop, Vorak the Fence followed her back to her hole and took everything she had."

"Oh," Dorna said again.

"If he goes to Wizard Street—well, the thing is, Ezak always tells some fancy story about where he got whatever it is he's trying to sell. The fences don't care, but if a magician knew Ezak was telling lies about where the talismans came from, and some magicians have magic that tells them when someone is lying, well, he might tell the magistrate, or the guardsmen. That would be bad."

"I see," Dorna said.

They walked on in silence for awhile after that, as the sun sank toward the western horizon. Then Dorna asked, "Why do you stay with him?"

Kel blinked. "With Ezak?"

"Yes."

"Because we're friends. He takes care of me."

"It seems to me that *you* take care of *him*."

"Sometimes," Kel agreed.

"It sounds as if he gets you both into trouble a lot."

"Sometimes," Kel repeated.

"You might do better on your own," she said.

Kel shook his head. "Ezak is smarter than I am. I need him."

"No, he isn't smarter. He's an idiot."

"He's *always* been smarter," Kel insisted.

"When you were kids, maybe—he's older than you?"

"A couple of years, at least. We don't really know exactly how old he is."

"Well, you aren't kids any more, and believe me, Kel, you're smarter than he is."

Kel shook his head and said nothing.

A moment later he said, "He's bigger than me. He protects me."

"You wouldn't *need* so much protecting if he wasn't getting you in trouble!"

"He's my friend."

"Sooner or later, he's going to get one of you killed."

Kel didn't answer.

The sun was down, and the light was fading, so that Kel no longer saw every rock or rathole and stumbled occasionally as they marched on across the fields, when Dorna suddenly said, "You know there's still plenty of sorcery in the wagon back at the Golden Rooster, don't you?"

"Yes," Kel said.

"So you know I'm going to use it to hunt him down and get my things back?"

"Yes," Kel said again.

"I warned him."

"Yes, you did."

She stared at him for a moment, then said, "For your sake, I won't kill him if I can avoid it."

"Thank you," Kel said. He pointed at a farmhouse ahead, where a lamp had just flared up in a window. "Could we stop there for the night?"

"We can ask," Dorna said. "I wonder where Ezak will sleep?"

"Probably in a ditch somewhere," Kel said. "He doesn't have any money."

Dorna grimaced; Kel could see that, even in the dim light.

"Don't worry," he said. "He's used to it."

TEN

The farmer had been happy to provide food and lodging for a price that was only mildly outrageous; Kel thought it was a very good thing that Dorna had kept her purse on her belt, and not put it in the canvas bag with her magic. Kel had hoped that the obviously-magical *fil drepessis* might intimidate their host into accommodating them for free, or at least very cheaply, but instead it appeared to have the opposite effect. Even though the farmer had no idea what it was, and neither Dorna nor Kel would tell him, he seemed to think that its presence meant that his guests were magicians, despite their claims to the contrary. Everyone knew magicians were all rich and could afford to pay any amount asked. Dorna was too tired, and too angry at Ezak, to be in the mood for negotiations, and agreed on the bill with only minimal haggling.

Once the terms had been determined Kel and Dorna ate, bathed, and then settled onto the farmer's bed, while their host made do with a blanket and a pile of straw. The bed was somewhat crowded with both of them in it, quite aside from Kel's discomfort with the impropriety of the situation, but Kel had slept in cramped quarters before. As for the two of them sharing, Dorna told Kel he was being silly to worry about it, and they were sufficiently exhausted that not only were they both quickly asleep, but they both slept late.

Kel felt much better after a good night's sleep and a good breakfast, and Dorna seemed equally pleased, even though their host had charged them almost three times what they would have paid at a good inn. The farmer also provided directions to Shepherd's Well at no additional cost, and they set out around mid-morning.

This proved to be the warmest day of the year so far, and Kel would have been happy to spend it sitting in the shade somewhere, but Dorna maintained a brisk pace, and he kept up without complaint.

They reached the Golden Rooster an hour or two after noon, and found Irien waiting for them in the inn's cool interior. Her reaction upon seeing Dorna walk in with the *fil drepessis* under her arm was an outburst of relief, and she flung herself at her friend with such enthusiasm that Kel had to snatch the big talisman away so that it wouldn't be sent flying. The thought of accidentally triggering it and setting off another chase terrified him.

"You're safe!" Irien exclaimed, as she embraced the sorcerer's widow.

"I'm fine," Dorna said, pulling away. "Has Ezak been here?"

"What happened to your hair?" Irien demanded, as she looked at Dorna and saw where Northern sorcery had sliced away a large hank of her hair.

"Nothing," Dorna lied. "Is Ezak here?"

"I didn't expect you to be gone so long!"

"I know; I'm sorry. It took longer than I expected. Have you seen Ezak?"

The repetition of the question finally penetrated Irien's enthusiasm. "Wasn't he with you?" she asked.

"He was. He ran off. Did he come here?"

"I don't think so," Irien said.

"Why are you in *here*, then? Is someone watching the wagon?"

"Oh," Irien said. "I...I paid a local boy..."

"Come on." Dorna turned and headed back out the inn door, then toward the stableyard, with Irien and Kel close behind. Kel was still lugging the *fil drepessis*.

A boy of about ten, in a brownish tunic and black cowhide breeches, was sitting on the driver's bench of Dorna's wagon, whittling at a good-sized chunk of wood; he looked up at the sound of approaching footsteps, lowered the wood, and brandished his knife. Then he recognized Irien and lowered the blade, as well. "Are they with you?" he called. He had a surprisingly loud voice.

"Ducks and rabbits," Irien called back. Kel looked at her in confusion. "It's a password," Irien explained to Dorna. "If I'd said anything else, he was to raise the alarm."

"Clever," Dorna said.

Irien turned up a palm. "Simple enough," she said. Then she called to the boy, "Has anyone else been here? Perhaps a young man?"

"No," the boy said. "It's been as dull as sheep."

"Damn," Dorna said.

"Isn't that good?" Kel asked. "It means he didn't steal anything more."

"It *also* means we don't know where he went, and there may not be enough traces left here for a tracker to follow."

"He went home to Ethshar," Kel said.

Dorna stopped and turned to look at him. "You said before that he'd meet you there. How do you know?"

Kel turned up an empty palm. "Where else would he go? He doesn't *know* anywhere but Ethshar."

"He doesn't?"

"No."

"You're sure?"

"I've known him all my life," Kel said. "So far as I know, the first time he ever set foot outside the city walls was no more than three sixnights ago, when we went to look for your village."

"Which Ethshar?" Irien asked.

"Ethshar of the Sands," Kel replied.

"We knew that," Dorna said.

"Did we?" Irien asked sharply. "How do we know that they told us the truth? How do we know he's telling us the truth now? Every word could be lies!"

Dorna smiled. "Irien, do you think they're *smart* enough to lie about *all* of it?"

Irien glanced at Kel, then grimaced. "Maybe not," she acknowledged.

Kel thought she expected him to be insulted, but he wasn't; Ezak always said it was useful if your target under-estimated you. Besides, Kel didn't think he *could* have maintained so elaborate a lie. That was one reason he tried not to talk when he didn't need to. He had inadvertently given away too many schemes and secrets in the past.

Then they were at the wagon, where Dorna threw back the cover and began poking through the contents. The boy on the driver's bench watched with intense interest. "Is that magic stuff?" he asked.

"Sorcery," Dorna said, as she fished out another of the golden-boot-heel talismans. "It's all sorcery."

"Dorna," Irien said, "you don't have your bag."

"That's right," Dorna said. Kel was amazed she didn't say something a little more pointed, where it had taken Irien so long to notice the bag's absence.

"Ezak stole it?"

"Yes."

"How?"

Dorna stopped rummaging and straightened up, but did not look at her friend. Instead she let out a long, slow breath and said, "I'll tell you later."

"It was my fault," Kel said.

Dorna turned, startled, to look at him. "No, it wasn't," she said.

"I shouldn't have left him there."

"*I* shouldn't have left him there!" Dorna replied. "I was the one with the weapon."

Kel tightened his lips and did not respond. Dorna stared at him for a moment, then said, "Give me that."

Kel handed her the *fil drepessis*, and she heaved it up into the wagon. Then she pushed a few things around, pulled the cloth covering back into place, and turned to face Kel and Irien. "You're absolutely sure he'd go to Ethshar of the Sands?"

"Yes," Kel said. "He doesn't know anywhere else."

"You don't think he might realize we'd look for him there, and try somewhere else?"

Kel considered that, thinking carefully about how Ezak would behave, then shook his head. Ezak had had enemies looking for him before, and had never tried to leave the city. "Ethshar is very big, and he knows it much better than you do. He has a hundred hiding places, and he wouldn't know how to find a fence anywhere else."

"Ethshar it is, then," Dorna said. "There's no sense in putting it off. Irien, pay this fine young man whatever you promised him, give him an extra two bits from me, and then let us get out of here."

"I need to pay the innkeeper, too, and fetch things from our room…"

"Then go do it," Dorna snapped. "I want to get moving." She held out the boot-heel-shaped talisman and rubbed her thumb along one side of it; Kel thought he could see something shift and twist on its surface as she did.

"Can you find him?" Kel asked.

"Maybe," she said. "There's *something* in that direction." She pointed toward one side of the yard, the side Kel judged to be in the general direction of Ethshar.

Irien fished coins from a purse on her belt and gave them to the boy as Dorna fiddled with her talisman. The boy accepted the money happily, jumped down from the wagon, then stood to one side, watching; he obviously found these people far more interesting than anything else in Shepherd's Well.

Irien then turned and headed to the inn while Dorna went back to the wagon and straightened the cover. Kel stood aside, and glanced at the boy.

"I'm Bern," the boy said.

"I'm called Kel," Kel replied.

"Are you a magician?"

Kel shook his head. "No."

"*She* is, though?" Bern jerked his head toward Dorna.

"Sort of," Kel said. "Her husband was a sorcerer."

"Was? Did he lose his magical powers?"

"He died."

"Did one of his spells go wrong?"

"No."

"Then what happened?"

Kel turned up an empty hand. "He just died."

"Was he hundreds of years old?"

Kel shook his head.

"I heard that magicians can live for hundreds of years."

"That's wizards," Kel said. "I don't think sorcerers do."

Dorna looked up from the wagon. She had obviously overheard some of the conversation. "*Some* of them live a long time," she said as she turned around. "Not as long as wizards, but over a century."

"Oh," Bern said.

"My husband Nabal didn't, though," Dorna continued. "He was sixty-three when he died. His heart stopped."

"Oh," Bern said again.

"He had magic that might have saved him if he'd ever thought to use it on himself," Dorna added. "But he didn't."

"I'm sorry," Kel said.

"He didn't know there was anything wrong. If he had, he could have healed his heart, the way I healed your friend's head," she said, looking directly at Kel.

Kel could not think of anything to say, and just looked back at Dorna. Bern cast a nervous glance at Kel, and decided not to say anything, either.

"He thought he had plenty of time," Dorna said. "So did I."

"Have you healed *your* heart?" Kel asked.

"I checked," she said. "It doesn't need healing. Not that way, anyway."

"I hope it heals the other way," Kel said.

Dorna stared at him for a moment, then said, "I'll get the oxen." Her voice sounded oddly unsteady.

While Dorna was gathering draft animals and Irien was settling the bill, Kel found himself and Bern in the stableyard with the unguarded wagon—or at least, no one obvious was guarding it. He glanced at Bern. "Did you take anything from the wagon?"

Bern considered Kel for a moment, and then said, "No. Did you?"

"No. But my partner did."

"You have a partner?"

"Ezak of Ethshar. He got away with a whole bag of sorcery." Kel's voice rang with pride as he said that, but at the same time he was embarrassed.

Bern thought this over, looking from Kel to the wagon, and back again. "Where is he, then?"

"He got away," Kel repeated.

"But he's your partner?"

"Yes."

"Then why aren't you with him?"

"I…I was busy," Kel replied, his pride vanished.

"So he just left you with that woman?"

Kel paused before answering, "Yes."

"That doesn't sound like much of a partner. Is he going to come back for you?"

"No," Kel admitted. "But when I find him he'll give me a share of the loot."

"It sounded to me like the bossy one was going to find him for herself."

"Well…yes," Kel acknowledged. "But when Ezak gets away from her again, if there's any loot left, I'll get a share."

"Does *she* know that?"

Kel frowned. This conversation was not going the way he wanted it to. He had wanted to brag about being partners with someone clever enough to steal a bag full of magic, but this boy didn't seem very impressed. It was true that Kel didn't really think he would get a share of Ezak's loot, because he didn't expect Ezak to be able to sell it before Dorna found him and took it all back, but he hadn't expected Bern to realize that.

"I don't know," he said.

"She seems to trust you," Bern said. "Does she know you're the thief's partner?"

"Yes."

"Then why doesn't she have you locked up?"

"*I* didn't steal anything," Kel said. "I helped her get that fill-dirt-presses thing back. We blew up a Northern sorcery, too."

Bern frowned. "I don't understand," he said. "Are you on *her* side, or *your partner's* side?"

Kel blinked at the boy. "I don't know," he said. He was startled to realize that he really *didn't* know. Up until a few days ago he was always unquestionably on Ezak's side, in everything, but he *liked* Dorna, and she had treated him fairly—generously, even. No one else had ever done that.

"Kel!" Dorna's shout broke into Kel's thoughts and interrupted the conversation before Bern could say anything more. "Get over here and give me a hand with this harness!"

Kel hurried to help, and Bern followed him. When Kel glanced back at the boy, Bern smiled. "Yoking oxen is easier with more hands," he said. "It should be good for another two or three bits."

It was indeed good for another three bits. Twenty minutes later Bern stood in front of the inn, waving with one hand while the other clutched his pay, as Dorna and Irien drove their respective wagons out of the stableyard onto the road and turned them to the southeast, toward Ethshar of the Sands.

Kel was riding with Dorna on the lead wagon, and when they had gone perhaps half a mile she handed him the reins and said, "Here. Keep us on the road."

Kel took the lines and watched as Dorna fished out the boot-heel talisman. "There's a concentration of *gaja* ahead of us, in that direction," she said, pointing ahead and slightly to the right. "It's moving, so it's probably him."

Kel looked in the indicated direction. "There's a fence," he said. That side of the road was indeed lined with a rail fence for as far as he could see.

"I know. We'll stick to the road for now."

Driving the oxen did not take a great deal of concentration, so Kel had time to think as they rode on.

He thought Dorna was almost certainly going to catch up to Ezak eventually, and reclaim her stolen talismans. She had said she wouldn't kill Ezak, so after she had her bag back she would probably let them go—or maybe she would have Ezak flogged first, and *then* let them go. Kel winced at the idea of Ezak being flogged; having been through it himself, he knew how staggeringly painful and humiliating it was. He might have to spend a sixnight or so nursing Ezak back to health; he certainly couldn't afford to pay for healing magic, and he doubted anyone else was going to provide it.

But Dorna might be satisfied with just getting her things back. That would be nice. Then he and Ezak would go back to their old life, as it had been before Ezak's uncle told them about the dead sorcerer with a houseful of magic—stealing coins in taverns, running errands for a bit or two, and so on.

Kel looked around at the green fields stretching off in all directions, a flock of birds soaring in the blue sky ahead, a farmer with a tool of some kind poking at the ground off to the left, and for an instant he wondered if he really had to go back to living in alleys or attics, spending his nights grabbing for dropped coins in crowded taverns stinking of sweat and spilled beer.

But how could he possibly do anything else?

ELEVEN

They were nearing the great stone towers of Grandgate, the main entrance to Ethshar of the Sands, and Dorna was frowning as she tapped at her talisman. "It's somewhere over that way," she said, pointing to the left. "I can't tell whether it's in the city or not."

"Smallgate is in that direction," Kel said.

She glanced at him. "Smallgate," she said thoughtfully. "Is there an actual *gate* in Smallgate? A way into the city?"

"Of course," said Kel, startled. "Why else would they call it that?"

"Maybe because there *used* to be one, a couple of hundred years ago," Dorna answered. "Names don't always change when they should."

Kel could not argue with that. "There's a gate," he said. "It isn't always open, though."

"I didn't know Ethshar of the Sands *had* more than one gate," Dorna said. "Everyone uses Grandgate. Or arrives by sea."

"The highway only goes to Grandgate," Kel said.

Dorna considered this, looked at the towers ahead, and then at the talisman in her hand. "So how many gates *are* there?" she asked.

"Four."

"Grandgate, Smallgate—what are the others, Mediumgate and Tinygate?"

"Beachgate and Northgate," Kel said. He pointed to the west. "They're over that way."

Dorna looked in that direction, then shook her head. "We need to go south," she said. "I guess we're bound for Smallgate." She chirruped to the oxen and tugged on the reins, urging them off the highway onto one of the ill-defined lanes that led through the maze of huts and market stalls that lined the approaches to Grandgate.

Kel looked around worriedly. In particular, he looked back at the wagon, and at Irien's wagon behind Dorna's. He saw the locals watching as the wagons passed by, and saw that some of them were inching nearer. He turned and glanced ahead, and saw groups of children muttering among themselves.

"Stop," he said. "Stop right now."

"What?" Dorna had already been dividing her attention between the reins and her tracking talisman, and this new distraction seemed to be confusing her.

"Stop!" Kel shouted. "Stop here, and get your weapon out!" He drew his own belt-knife, wishing he had a club or a sword, or anything with more reach.

Dorna yanked on the reins, then turned and demanded, "What's wrong?"

"Get out your weapon *now*," Kel ordered, as he got to his feet. He saw Irien stop her own wagon, her oxen's noses only a foot or so from the back of Dorna's wagon, and he saw half a dozen men and women closing in behind.

"Get away!" Kel shouted. He pointed at Dorna. "She's a sorcerer, and if you touch either of these wagons, or anything in them, she'll blow your head off!"

Finally grasping the situation, Dorna stood as well, brandishing the black weapon that had destroyed the Northern sentry talisman. She did not speak.

"Blast anyone who gets too close," Kel said, as he sat down and grabbed the reins. He called over his shoulder, "Irien! Stay close!" Then he shook the reins and urged the oxen forward. Dorna swayed as the wagon started moving, but stayed upright and vigilant.

"It's almost two miles to Smallgate," Kel said. "We could double back to the highway."

"Is it like this the entire way?" Dorna asked, not looking down at him.

"I don't know," Kel said. "I never came outside the walls. When Ezak and I left we went out through Grandgate, and anyway, we didn't have anything worth stealing."

"Turn back," she said.

Kel nodded, and tugged at the reins, turning the oxen to the right, into the gap between a ragged blue tent and a rough wooden stall displaying old tools for sale. People who had been watching the whole thing reluctantly made way.

"*Hai*!" Dorna called, pointing her weapon at something behind them. Kel did not look, but urged the oxen forward, trying to coax more speed from the lumbering beasts.

A moment later they were back on the highway, and bound for Grandgate. The people who had been crowding close to the wagons had vanished, and after a final wary glance Dorna sat down—though Kel noticed she kept the weapon ready in her hand. Sweat gleamed on her brow, and while the weather was warm, Kel doubted it was entirely due to the heat.

"What was *that* about?" she asked.

"The city guard doesn't go there," Kel said. "They keep the highway clear, and everything inside the walls is under their protection, but that's all."

"So—what would have happened? Who are those people?"

Kel turned up an empty palm. "They're just people. Some of them don't have anywhere else to stay, so they live here. Some live in the city, or other places, but they come here to sell things. Sometimes it's things the guards wouldn't let them sell in the city markets. But they all steal things, if you give them a chance. They'll come up to the back of a wagon and grab whatever they can, then run with it. Usually it isn't anything valuable, so no one bothers to go after them."

Dorna considered this for a moment, then said, "Threatening to kill them seems excessive."

"They wouldn't listen to less," Kel said. "And if one of them got something from your wagon, and the others found out you have an entire wagon full of magic, they would have mobbed us and stolen everything."

"You seem very sure of this," Dorna said. "I thought you said you'd never been out here."

"I heard about what it was like out here," Kel said.

"You believed it?"

"It happens some places inside the walls, too."

"Where?"

"Smallgate."

"So you've seen people do that? Grab things off wagons?"

"I was one of them," Kel said.

Dorna did not say anything for a moment, but sat silently, the weapon in her hand, as they rode into the shadow of Grandgate's towers.

"I thought you said the guard protected people inside the walls," she said.

"They do," Kel said. "But they can't be everywhere at once, and I knew where to hide from them."

There were half a dozen soldiers in red and gold standing in front of the immense open gates, watching as civilians hurried in and out of the city; one of them waved to Kel, and he brought the wagon to a halt. The guardsman ambled toward them, spear in hand, sun glinting from his breastplate.

"So you stole things off wagons?" Dorna asked quietly.

"Yes," Kel said, hoping she would not say anything too incriminating once the soldier was in earshot.

"Ever get anything good?"

"Not really. This tunic I'm wearing is probably the best thing I ever stole that way."

She turned to stare at the old red tunic just as the guardsman trotted the last few steps and said, "*Hai*! What's in the wagon?"

Startled, Dorna looked from Kel to the guard. "What?"

Kel jerked his head toward Dorna. "It's hers," he said. "I'm just helping."

The soldier nodded. "So what have you got there?" he asked Dorna. He set the butt of his spear on the ground by his foot, and gestured at the wagon with his free hand.

Dorna looked helplessly at Kel.

"He just wants to know whether you're bringing anything illegal," Kel said, trying to sound reassuring. "They stop any wagon they don't recognize."

"How am I supposed to know what's illegal here?" Dorna asked uneasily.

Kel sighed. He turned to the guard. "She's a sorcerer's widow," he explained. "She's brought her husband's magic to sell."

The guard frowned. "Is any of it dangerous?"

"Yes," Kel said, before Dorna could react. She glared at him.

The soldier just nodded, then turned his head and bellowed over his shoulder, "Amdis! Get over here!"

"What are you *doing*?" Dorna hissed to Kel. "Why did you say that?"

"You don't want to lie," Kel said quietly. "Sometimes they have magic that can tell."

"So you just *tell him* that I have dangerous magic?"

"Yes," Kel answered, slightly puzzled at Dorna's obvious annoyance. "*That's* not illegal. Ethshar is *full* of dangerous magic."

"Oh," Dorna said. She straightened up and looked at the soldier, who smiled cheerfully at her. "Then what *is* illegal?"

"Swords, if you don't have a permit," Kel answered. "Unlicensed *oushka* in anything bigger than a bottle. Baby dragons. Poisonous fruit. Things like that."

"Listen to your friend," the guardsman said, grinning and shifting his weight to lean on his spear. "Sounds like he knows the rules."

"Oh," Dorna said again.

"There *are* rules about magic, but we don't handle those," the soldier explained. "That's up to the magicians. If you've got forbidden wizardry, the Wizards' Guild will let you know; if it's bad witchcraft, the Sisterhood will talk to you. Sorcery, I'm not sure who looks after that, or if there really *are* any rules. It's not my concern."

"I see."

"So, what *else* do you have in that wagon, besides sorcery?" the guardsman asked. "Anything we should know about?"

Dorna shook her head. "It's all sorcery," she said. "Everything else is in my friend's wagon." She pointed at Irien, who was talking to another soldier.

The guardsman straightened, picked up his spear, and pointed it past Dorna at her magical cargo. "*All* sorcery? That whole big wagon?"

"That's right."

The soldier frowned, then called, "Amdis, bring a friend!"

A moment later another soldier trotted up, spear in hand, and made a hasty bow. "Amdis of Cutler Street," he said. "I'll be escorting you. Do you know where you're going?"

He was smaller and younger than the first guardsman, though still bigger than either Dorna or Kel. Dorna glanced at Kel as the soldier who had originally interrogated them gave them a parting wave and moved on, leaving them in Amdis' care.

"No," Kel said.

"What is it you're carrying?" Amdis asked.

"Sorcery," Kel said. "A *lot* of sorcery."

"No wonder the sergeant thought you needed an escort. You're a sorcerer?"

"No," Kel said.

"My husband was," Dorna replied.

"But *you* aren't?"

"No. He died, and I inherited his magic, and I've come to sell it."

"Ah," Amdis said. "Do you want to store it in the city vaults until you find a place?"

Dorna looked at Kel. "Can we *do* that?"

Kel turned up an empty hand. "I don't know," he said. "I never had anything worth guarding."

"There's a fee," Amdis explained. "If you want to pay a little extra, the guards will be especially careful."

"Does that apply to our escort, as well?" Dorna asked.

Amdis spread empty hands. "I wouldn't mind a few extra bits. But I'll do my job either way. It's not required."

"The vaults aren't required either, are they?"

"No," Amdis admitted. "But honestly, unless you have protective spells on the wagon, I'd recommend using them. If you really have an entire wagon full of sorcery—well, *do* you have protective spells? You said you aren't a sorcerer; are you a wizard, or anything?"

"No," Dorna acknowledged. "And the protective spells— well, they aren't very effective." She glanced at Kel, who said nothing. He remembered the screaming talisman back in Shepherd's Well; he doubted that would discourage most of the thieves here in the city.

"Then I'd recommend the vaults."

Another soldier strode up just as Dorna asked, "Where are they?"

Amdis turned and pointed. "Under the north tower," he said.

"Here in Grandgate?"

"Sure. After all, it's mostly people going in and out of the city who need them."

That seemed to convince her, and twenty minutes later Kel, Dorna, Irien, and half a dozen soldiers were rolling the wagon down a ramp into an iron-lined stone vault, one of a row cut into the foundations of the immense north tower. The oxen had been switched to Irien's wagon and were waiting patiently on the street above, with yet another soldier watching them.

The lock that secured the vault door used three keys; two stayed with the tower's staff, and Dorna was given the third. She was offered the option of paying a wizard to put a sealing rune of one sort or another on the vault, as well, but she turned that down; quite aside from professional pride making her reluctant to use any magic other than sorcery, it would have added at least a round of silver to the price. The fee for the vault itself seemed quite reasonable—a mere six bits a day.

Filling out the paperwork took longer than getting the wagon in the vault, but an hour after arriving at the gate the three of them—Dorna, Irien, and Kel—were squeezed onto the driver's bench of Irien's wagon, rolling south on Wall Street and looking for a suitable inn.

Or rather, Irien was looking for a suitable inn. Dorna had her tracking talisman in hand, and was fiddling with it. She had kept that and the black weapon; Kel was unsure whether she had taken any other sorcery from her wagon.

"There's too much other magic here," she said. "It's getting confused."

"It can wait," Irien said. "What about that one?" She pointed at a signboard on a side-street, a few doors from Wall Street.

Kel leaned over and saw a the sign in question; it depicted three feathers above the words "Food—Drink—Lodging."

"I don't know it," he said.

Irien glanced at him. "I thought you used to steal purses in taverns."

Kel had almost never stolen entire purses, especially not in taverns, but he did not bother correcting her; he merely said, "Not that one. It's too close to the Grandgate barracks."

"That sounds like a *recommendation* to me."

Kel turned up an empty palm.

"Good enough," Irien said. She tugged the reins to turn the oxen.

"What? No, wait!" Dorna protested, looking up from her talisman. "My bag is *that* way!" She pointed directly down Wall Street.

"The inn is *that* way," Irien replied. "I think we need to arrange lodging before we do anything else."

"No!" Dorna said. "No, I could lose him."

"Couldn't Kel find him for you?"

Kel ducked at the suggestion. Dorna barely glanced at him as she said, "Not before he sells my talismans!"

Kel thought she was over-estimating Ezak's ability to fence magic, but did not say so.

"Dorna, I am *not* going to drive this wagon halfway across the city through these streets! *Look* at them!" She waved an arm to take in their surroundings.

Kel looked around.

This was Grandgate, not his home territory, but it was still reassuringly familiar. To their left was the Wall Street Field, where no permanent structures were permitted; this particular stretch held no structures at all because it was too close to Grandgate and the guard barracks, and therefore had soldiers traipsing across it at all hours, discouraging the erection of tents or other temporary shelters. To their right were houses, shops, and taverns, mostly catering to a military clientele— vintners, armorers, gaming halls, and the like. Behind them on the left, just beyond Wall Street Field, rose the immense north tower; ahead on the left, beyond the field, was the inner gatehouse. Directly ahead of them, past the gatehouse, was the broad open expanse of Grandgate Market, jammed with carts, market stalls, farmers, merchants, and customers. It all smelled of smoke and sweat and dirt, and the sounds of footsteps and calling voices and rattling wheels filled the air. None of it looked at all out of the ordinary to Kel.

There were hundreds of people in sight, going about their business. Dozens of them were driving various carts or wagons. Kel was not quite sure what Irien found so unappealing about driving here, but then, she *was* from a tiny village; maybe this was too crowded for her.

"Fine," Dorna said. "Stop here, then, and Kel and I will go on on foot. It'll probably be faster anyway."

"But...I don't..." Irien said.

"You book us a room at that inn you like, and take care of the wagon, and we'll find you there later."

"Dorna, I—"

"Go on!" She looked up from her talisman long enough to spot the signboard. "The Three Feathers, across from the tower where the vaults are. We'll find it." She stood up, a trifle unsteadily, while the vehicle was still moving.

Irien halted the oxen and watched unhappily as Dorna awkwardly climbed down—awkwardly, because she was keeping her talisman in hand and in sight the entire time.

Kel hesitated.

"Come on, Kel," Dorna called, her gaze still focused on her magical guide. "I may need you. You know the city, and I don't."

Kel hurried to the step, but just before he leapt to the ground he turned back to Irien and said, "I'm sorry."

Then he was following Dorna at a trot, south through Grandgate Market, as Irien drove the wagon into the side-street.

TWELVE

From Grandgate Market Dorna led the way down Soldiertown Street, then hesitated where Barracks Street forked off to the left. She looked at Kel. He pointed to the right, and they continued down Soldiertown, drawing curious glances from passersby.

As they continued almost due south through Soldiertown, Dorna grew steadily more agitated. Finally she stopped, and looked around wildly.

"We're going the wrong way!" she said. "He's in *that* direction!" She pointed ahead and to the left.

"He's probably somewhere in Smallgate," Kel said, nodding.

"But none of the streets *go* that direction!"

"No, they don't," Kel agreed, puzzled.

"Why *not*?"

This question struck Kel as rather like asking why water is wet; the streets went where the streets went, and there wasn't anything anyone could do about it. "Most of the streets in Soldiertown go either north and south, or east and west," he said. "Except for the alleys off Gambler Street, there aren't any curves or diagonals between Whore Street and Smallgate."

She glared at him.

"There are plenty of crooked streets in Smallgate," Kel offered helpfully. "That's how you'll know when we're in Smallgate, and not in Soldiertown anymore."

"Then how are we supposed to get to where Ezak has my things, if none of the streets go there?"

"He's probably somewhere in Smallgate," Kel repeated.

"Yes, but how do we *get* to Smallgate?"

"Straight down Soldiertown to Midway Street is the easiest," Kel said.

"What's the *fastest*?"

"Oh, I don't…I mean…" Kel looked around for a way to escape, but Dorna grabbed his shoulder.

"Show me," she demanded.

Kel bit his lower lip, then nodded. "This way," he said.

They turned left on Gambler Street, then right on Cheaters' Alley, where Kel popped the hidden latch on Bennimin the Lender's back gate, so they could cut through a nameless courtyard, ducking under a clothesline and then out a smoke-blackened passage to emerge on Armorer Street, which they followed four blocks further south, past homes and second-hand shops and a tinker's workshop—the actual armorers were all further to the north. A dry culvert, another courtyard, and another narrow nameless alley brought them to Archer Street, where Dorna's talisman indicated their target was now almost directly south of them, straight down the road, less than half a mile away; the sorcerer's widow was visibly relieved by this discovery. "It's a good thing we left the wagon with Irien," she said, glancing back at the route they had followed. "But it's straight from here." She smiled.

Kel was not quite so cheerful about it. He was somewhat surprised they had not encountered any real obstacles or hazards yet—the shortcuts they had used were not always so cooperative. He knew that "straight" did not always mean "easy," and in fact their route probably wasn't going to be straight at all. Archer Street ended at Smallgate Street, just north of a tangle of alleys and byways that Dorna would probably find incomprehensible—not to mention dangerous. That was Kel's home neighborhood, and where he thought they were likely to find Ezak, but the prospect of bringing a woman there, a small woman who did not know the city or its customs and who did not look at all intimidating, did not appeal to him. She did have her magical weapon, but the people most likely to jump her might not recognize it as a weapon at all. Her only visible protection would be Kel, and Kel did not think his presence was going to seriously deter anyone—especially after dark, and the afternoon shadows were lengthening ominously. As he watched, he saw a woman in a gauzy red skirt step out to light the lantern above her elaborately-painted door.

Dorna looked at her talisman, ignoring the locals. "There's something over that way that's interfering," she said, pointing to the west.

"Wizard Street is about eight blocks in that direction," Kel said.

"That would account for it," she acknowledged.

They marched on, past Uncle Vezalis' house; Kel did not point it out, and the talisman apparently did not react to it. Ten minutes after emerging from the alley they reached the intersection of Archer and Smallgate, where Archer Street ended. Dorna stared at the tenement ahead of them as if its existence was a personal affront, then looked down at the talisman. "It's still pointing straight ahead," she said. "About...two hundred yards, maybe?"

Kel nodded. "This way," he said, turning right.

Dorna reluctantly followed, keeping an eye on the talisman and glancing now and then at the two- and three-story buildings that lined the south side of Smallgate Street.

"Smallgate Street doesn't actually go to the gate," Kel remarked, trying to distract her. "It ends at Wall Street maybe a quarter-mile from the gatehouse. It's just called Smallgate Street because it leads straight from the Palace to the district of Smallgate. The only streets at the gate itself are Wall Street and Landsend Street."

"All right," Dorna said, obviously not listening.

Kel sighed. "This way," he said, turning left into an alley.

Dorna followed, still focused on the golden boot-heel as Kel led her around the corner into the shadowed passage. She was oblivious to their surroundings, trusting Kel and her sorcery to guide her.

"Dorna?" Kel said, as they walked on.

"Right," she said, staring at the talisman.

"*Dorna*!"

She looked up, annoyed. "What?"

"You might want to be less obvious about that thing you're holding."

Dorna looked around, suddenly realizing that they were in a cramped, crooked alley between two buildings that had seen not merely better days, but better centuries. The plaster walls on either side were webbed with cracks and patches, and the patches themselves were cracked and patched—or sometimes *not* patched; wattle was exposed several places. The ground beneath their feet was packed garbage, not sand. The few windows within ten feet of the ground were tightly shuttered, or completely bricked up. The windows on the upper floors were more varied—open, closed, shuttered, barred, or broken—and she could see at least two pairs of eyes staring down at them from open casements. Little sunlight managed to find its way through the narrow gap between the roofs overhead. There were no other pedestrians in sight.

"This isn't a safe place for outsiders," Kel said. "Or for anyone, really."

"Oh," Dorna said. Instead of putting the talisman out of sight, though, as Kel had hoped she would, she merely switched it to her other hand and drew the black weapon from her belt and held that ready.

"It's going to get worse," Kel said.

She threw him a glance. "Why? Isn't there a safer route?"

"To where we usually live when Ezak's uncle won't let us in? No."

"No?"

"We needed a place so bad slavers wouldn't come in and catch us while we were sleeping."

She stared at him for a moment, then said, "Oh." She looked around the alley again. "How do you know he isn't at his uncle's house?"

"Because we went right past it, and your magic didn't point at it."

Dorna looked at her talisman, then at Kel. "We did?"

Kel nodded. "Uncle Vezalis lives back on Archer Street," he said, pointing back the way they had come. "A block north of Smallgate Street. I don't think Ezak would trust his uncle with stolen magic in the house."

"Oh."

"I think I know where Ezak is, though."

"Go on, then," she said, gesturing with the weapon.

Kel went, leading the way through a broken gate at the back of the alley, across a shadowy courtyard that stank of things Kel did not care to think about, along a stretch of alleyway that had been walled off and no longer connected to any other streets, through the ruins of a building where the roof had fallen in years earlier, along another alley, and then down a set of steep steps into a dim, damp, stone-walled tunnel. The sandy floor squashed wetly beneath their feet.

Now that she had been alerted to the situation, Dorna grew more apprehensive as this journey through the maze of Smallgate wound on; in that first alley at least the eyes watching them from those upstairs windows had been human. By the time they crossed the ruin the only living creatures she saw were rats and spiders, and the rats were bolder than any she had ever encountered, staring at her, making no move to hide or flee.

"How can a place like this exist in Ethshar?" she whispered, as she ducked into the tunnel. "A place this deserted and decrepit?"

Kel looked back at her, startled. "It can't *all* be palaces," he said.

"I know that, but *this*..."

"We wanted a place the slavers couldn't get us," Kel said. "Somewhere with more privacy than the Wall Street Field."

"Well, you found *that*," Dorna said.

They were far enough into the tunnel now that the only faint light came from her gently glowing talisman. Kel was feeling his way along one wall; then he stopped, and whispered, "What does your sorcery say?"

"What? Oh." She peered at her magical boot-heel. Then she pointed. "Five yards that way." She held up the talisman so Kel could see her finger in its light.

"That's what I thought," he said. "Wait here."

"What, *wait*? Are you..." But then Kel was gone, and she was alone in the tunnel.

Ezak had long ago cleaned and oiled the hinges on the secret door into the old cellar, and Kel had been careful to keep them in good shape, so he was able to slip in without a sound, but that had been wasted effort; Ezak had the shutters to the air-shaft open, and enough of the setting sun's light made its way down the shaft to dimly illuminate most of the room's familiar confines, from the sand spilling through the crumbling east wall to the pile of rags in the northwest corner where Kel sometimes slept. Kel was plainly visible to anyone in the room.

So was Ezak. He was crouched ten feet from the door, holding a knife ready to throw, looking directly at Kel. For a moment Kel froze.

Then Ezak relaxed. "Oh, it's you!" he said. He smiled, and tossed the knife aside. "It's good to see you, Kel! I thought you were killed in that explosion!"

"I'm fine," Kel said. He looked around, and immediately spotted Dorna's bag; Ezak had made no attempt to hide it. It was sitting on the floor, midway between the door and the air-shaft. It looked just as full as Kel remembered it; Ezak had clearly not yet sold much, if any, of its contents.

Ezak noticed his gaze. "It's still all there," he said. "I looked through it when I made camp, but I couldn't make any sense of any of those things. I didn't do much experimentation; I didn't want anything to start screaming. I'm planning to take a few of them to Wizard Street tomorrow, and see what they tell me. I'm going to say I found them in the ruins of a sorcerer's house after an explosion, I think. Or maybe the sorcerer should be my grandfather, so I'll have a real claim to them, and not just salvage rights?"

"That sounds good," Kel said.

"So what happened back there? What exploded? Was Dorna killed?"

"The Northern sentry thing exploded," Kel said. "When Dorna blasted it with her husband's sorcery."

"She died, though, didn't she? Did you get the fill-dirt-presses back, or was it smashed, too?"

"We got it back," Kel said.

"We?" Ezak was suddenly wary.

"She wasn't killed," Kel said, as he swung the door behind him wide, letting the dim light spill out into the tunnel beyond.

Dorna stepped in, the black weapon in her hand. She pointed it at Ezak.

"You have some of my belongings," she said.

Ezak stared at her for only an instant before diving for the canvas bag, grabbing it up, and cradling it in his arm as he scrambled for the cellar's other exit. Kel had not yet decided what he should do about that when the weapon went off.

This time Kel was upright and watching, not diving for the grass; he saw the eerie blue gobbet of magic that shot from the talisman, struck the stone wall behind Ezak, and exploded. Kel closed his eyes, but there was no blinding white flash following the blue flash this time, and the sound was loud, like a sledgehammer shattering a stone block into gravel, but not the earth-shaking roar that the Northern device's destruction had produced. Apparently most of that explosion's power had come from the Northern magic, rather than the weapon that destroyed it.

Ezak screamed, dropped the bag, and fell to his knees on the sandy floor. "Don't kill me!" he said.

"Get away from the bag," Dorna said.

Ezak shoved the bag toward her, then backed away. "Why did you bring her here?" he asked Kel.

Kel did not answer; he simply stood and watched as Dorna crossed the room, snatched up her bag, and slung it on her shoulder. She dropped the boot-heel talisman into the bag, but kept the weapon ready in her hand.

"Thank you," she said, as she straightened up. "Kel asked me not to kill you, so for his sake, I won't. I won't even turn you over to the magistrates. But if you ever try to take anything of mine again, I *will* kill you. You understand that?"

Ezak nodded vigorously.

Then for a moment the three of them remained where they were—Kel standing by the door to the tunnel, Dorna standing in the middle of the room with her bag and weapon, Ezak kneeling near the hole in the wall where one could climb up to the next level—each waiting for someone else to do or say something. Finally, Dorna turned and headed back toward the tunnel. "Come on," she said.

"What?" the two young men said simultaneously.

"Not you," Dorna said to Ezak. "Him." She pointed at Kel.

"Me?"

"Yes! I need you to show me the way out of this place."

"Oh," Kel said, hurrying to follow her through the door. He had not realized she was one of those people who could not reliably retrace her steps. He knew such people existed, and had met them before, but he did not really understand them; he might not always know where he was, but anywhere in the city he always knew how he got there, and how to get back out. It was part of his nature.

But Dorna wasn't from Ethshar, she was from a little village somewhere, and her nature apparently differed from his. Besides, she had been so intent on her talisman that she probably hadn't really seen the route.

Once out of the room Kel took the lead. Neither of them spoke as they trudged back out and up the steps to the alley.

Dorna paused to glance up at the narrow strip of sky visible above them; it was noticeably darker than when they had come the other way. Then she turned to Kel, who was watching her. "I could probably have found my own way out, especially now I have my bag back, but I wanted to talk to you."

That was mildly surprising. Kel looked at her expectantly.

"You thought I was going to just go off and leave you here, didn't you?" she asked.

She seemed to want an answer. "Yes," he said.

"I couldn't do that. I couldn't just walk away and leave you in a place like this."

Kel looked around. The alley was a rough, ruinous place, but it was one he knew well. "I *live* here," he said. "Sometimes, anyway."

"Well, you shouldn't."

He could think of no sensible reply to that, and blinked silently at her.

"I'm going to open a tea shop," she said. "I'm going to import my favorite teas from the Small Kingdoms. I used to buy them from a trader named Vezalis who came to deal with Nabal; I'd ask him to bring me a new variety each trip he made, and to bring more of the ones I liked. I hadn't known there were so many kinds until I met him!"

"That's Ezak's uncle," Kel said. He had no idea why she was telling him about her plans, but he thought she might want to know.

"What?" That seemed to have jarred her out of her planned speech.

"Vezalis, the trader your husband dealt with. He's Ezak's uncle. That was how we found you."

She stared at him. "You're serious? I thought it was just a coincidence that they were both named Vezalis."

"Yes. The trader is Ezak's uncle."

"That *stupid*, troublesome…" She stopped abruptly, took a deep breath, let it out slowly, then said, "Never mind that. My point is, I'm going to open a tea shop."

Kel nodded. She had already said that.

"I'm going to spend a lot of my time dealing with tea merchants, and trying out different blends."

Kel nodded again. He knew almost nothing about running a tea shop, and in fact had never seen a tea shop, but this sounded reasonable.

"I'll need an assistant to look after the shop when I'm busy elsewhere. I'd like to hire you as my assistant."

Kel blinked; at first the words didn't seem to make sense. Eventually he managed to work out their meaning, but it still didn't seem reasonable. "But I'm a *thief*," he said. "No one hires a thief!"

"You wouldn't *be* a thief anymore," Dorna said. "You'd be a tea shop assistant."

That was too bizarre to grasp immediately, but Dorna was looking at him, clearly expecting a response. "I don't know," he said.

"The position would include room and board, and pay a round a sixnight to start," she said.

"Room and board?" He glanced back at the tunnel mouth, remembering the room they had just visited, where he had so often lived.

She nodded. "A room above the shop, and at least three meals a day," she said.

That knocked all thought of the room out of his head. Kel had never in his life eaten *three* meals a day; he had trouble comprehending such luxury. He stared at her, only just barely keeping his jaw from dropping.

"Why don't you give it a try?" Dorna said. "You can always quit if you don't like it."

Kel tried to imagine how someone could dislike eating regularly and sleeping indoors, and decided maybe *someone* could, but he was not that someone.

On the other hand, he knew someone who would look on this with a great deal of suspicion. "What about Ezak?" he asked.

She shook her head. "I'm only offering to hire *you*, Kel. You helped me when you could, and you've been as honest with me as a thief could be." She smiled wryly at that, then continued, "You're smarter than you realize, and I think you deserve a chance to use your wits for something better than stealing old clothes."

"But Ezak helped me," Kel said. "He's *always* helped me."

"But he stole from *me*. And he did nothing to help me *or* you after he sent the *fil drepessis* off looking for something to fix."

Kel hesitated.

Dorna saw his uncertainty and sighed. "Think about it," she said. "For now, get me out of here and back to the Three Feathers before it's too dark to see where we're going."

That was something Kel could understand and accept. "This way," he said.

By the time they got back to Grandgate and found Irien sitting in a quiet corner of the inn, Kel had made up his mind. Three meals a day! A dry room! *And* some money! How could he resist?

He couldn't. He didn't. He was hired on the spot, and given his own room at the inn at Dorna's expense.

He hoped Ezak wouldn't be too upset.

THIRTEEN

Kel had never realized how *complicated* starting a business was.

Irien took charge of finding a suitable location, while Dorna set about selling some of her husband's magic to fund the tea shop. Both of them used Kel as an errand boy, a job he had done before, but it was different this time—he didn't need to hold out his hand for a coin after each errand, and at the end of the day he sat down to a generous supper without worrying about how to pay for it, or where he would sleep.

He also served as a local guide for Dorna as she roamed up and down Wizard Street, talking to sorcerers and sorcerers' suppliers, gathering references and making appointments, and dickering over prices. He sometimes accompanied Irien as she traveled around the city, talking to landlords and property owners and magistrates and tax collectors about what spaces might be available for rent or purchase, what debts might be attached to them, and so on. He went along on several visits to the city vaults under the north barracks, and helped carry various sorceries to prospective buyers. Every night, when his work was done, he slept in a good bed at the Three Feathers, a bed he had all to himself, with no rats or roaches or centipedes around.

It was nice to have all that space and comfort, but sometimes at night he missed Ezak, and wondered where he was and what he was doing. Dorna and Irien kept Kel too busy to go back to Smallgate and check.

A sixnight after his return to Ethshar, Dorna informed Kel that he was now going to escort her to Vezalis' house, so that she could make arrangements for the trader to supply the shop with the teas Dorna wanted.

"I can show you which house it is," he said.

"I want you to talk to him with me, too."

"That might not be a good idea," Kel warned her. "He doesn't like me."

"That doesn't matter," Dorna said. "This is business."

Kel did not find that entirely convincing, but he did not argue further. He led Dorna back to Archer Street, but this time without any shortcuts—since Kel knew where they were going, they turned onto Archer at its northern end, in Grandgate, and walked it for the full length of Soldiertown, with no need to dodge through alleys and courtyards. When they neared Vezalis' house, Kel pointed it out. It was much like the other houses on the street—two stories with a steep-gabled attic, half-timbered, with painted plaster between the heavy wooden beams. The paintings on the trader's house were of ships under full sail, though, rather than the more customary gardens and crockery.

"It's not very big," Dorna remarked.

Kel turned up an empty palm. He was no judge of house sizes; they all seemed big to him.

"You're sure that's it?"

Kel nodded.

"All right," Dorna said. "Come on." She marched toward the door.

"Maybe I should wait here," Kel said, staying in the middle of the street.

Dorna stopped and beckoned to him. "No," she said. "You're coming with me. I told you that. You work for me, and you'll probably need to deal with him later, so you might as well get used to it."

Reluctantly, Kel followed her.

This would be the first time he ever approached Vezalis the Merchant with anyone other than Ezak present. It would be the first time he had come to this house when he was neither accompanying Ezak, nor looking for Ezak. He was not at all sure how Ezak's uncle would take that; would he think Kel was a traitor, abandoning the friend who had raised him?

Dorna waited on the front step until Kel came up behind her, then knocked loudly on the big red door. Kel waited apprehensively.

"He may not be home," he said, when no one answered Dorna's knock immediately. "He travels a lot."

"I know that," Dorna said, annoyed. "Does anyone else stay here when he's traveling?"

Kel hesitated. "He told me not to say."

Dorna glanced back at him. "Does he have any family?"

"Just Ezak."

"Does Ezak live here when his uncle's away, then?"

"No!" Kel said. "Uncle Vezalis wouldn't trust him that much."

Dorna snorted. "His own *uncle* doesn't trust him alone in the house?"

"His uncle knows him better than anyone."

Dorna laughed, then abruptly stopped, staring over Kel's shoulder.

Kel turned, and saw Ezak's uncle standing several yards away, watching the two of them warily. He was a big, burly man in a fraying velvet tunic and well-worn boots, but he seemed in no hurry to confront the short, skinny pair on the steps of his home.

"Vezalis!" Dorna called, waving. "I need to speak to you!"

Vezalis sighed, and walked toward them. Halfway there he cocked his head to one side. "Do I know you?" he said.

"Dorna the Clever," Dorna answered. "Nabal the Sorcerer's wife. I mean, widow."

"Oh!" The trader quickened his pace and held out a hand. Kel started at learning Dorna's full name for the first time—up until now she had called herself only "Dorna the Sorcerer's Widow" in his hearing. But then, he supposed that it would not be wise to call oneself "the Clever" in front of people you were going to be haggling with. "I never expected to see you *here*!" Vezalis said.

Dorna took his hand and said, "With my husband gone, I had no reason to stay in the village."

"Of course," Vezalis said. He looked warily at Kel. "You know this boy?" he asked.

"More or less," Dorna replied. "He and your nephew Ezak tried to steal some of my late husband's sorcery."

"Oh," Vezalis said, his expression more resigned than surprised. "I'm afraid I'm not responsible—"

Dorna shook her head. "That's not why I'm here," she interrupted. "He works for me now."

Vezalis stepped back. "*Works* for you?"

"Yes."

"But you know he's a thief?"

"He *was* a thief. Now he's my assistant."

"I… That's very generous of you." He threw a quick glance at Kel, who looked back defiantly.

"He's been earning his keep."

Vezalis gave Kel an uncertain look; Kel guessed the trader wanted to hear another side of the story. He did not say anything, though.

"Is Ezak working for you, as well?" the merchant asked.

"Certainly not! I wouldn't trust him for a moment."

Vezalis' expression was frankly puzzled, but before he could say anything more Dorna continued, "I've come about those teas you sold me."

"What about them?" Vezalis asked warily. "Was there a problem?"

"No, not at all. In fact, I was hoping you could supply me with more—*much* more."

For the first time, Vezalis smiled. "Oh?"

"Yes. I'm opening a tea shop over in Nightside, at the corner of Aristocrat and Harbor Streets, and I need someone who can keep me stocked with all those lovely varieties you used to bring me at my husband's shop."

"A tea shop?" He smiled, and clapped his hands together. "An entire *shop*? Wonderful! I'm sure something can be arranged."

"When would you like to *make* those arrangements? Might I come in?"

"Oh," Vezalis said. His smile vanished as he glanced at the still-closed door. "No, I'm afraid this is not a good time. Might I perhaps come by the shop, say, this afternoon?"

Dorna shook her head. "The shop is still being readied. Are you sure this isn't a good time?"

"Very sure."

"Then perhaps you could meet me at the Three Feathers, in Grandgate, this evening after sunset? And bring samples."

"I can do that," Vezalis agreed. "The Three Feathers?"

"On Gatehouse Lane, off Wall Street north of the market."

"I can find it."

"Good! Then I'll see you there." Dorna offered her hand again, then stepped back off the stoop and headed up Archer Street.

Kel started to follow her, but Vezalis called, "Kel! Wait a minute!"

Kel stopped, and turned back to Ezak's uncle. He was actually glad to be called back; he wanted to ask after Ezak.

"What's going on?" Vezalis asked quietly, with a glance at Dorna. "What are you two up to?"

"I'm helping her open a tea shop," Kel said.

"No, I meant you and Ezak. What are you up to?"

"Nothing. I haven't seen Ezak in a sixnight. Hasn't he been to see *you?*"

"Yes, he has, but when I asked where you were he said it didn't concern me."

Kel turned up an empty palm.

"Are you two all right?"

"I'm fine. I don't know about Ezak."

Vezalis glanced at Dorna, waiting for Kel ten yards up the street. "Are you two planning to rob her?" he asked quietly.

"No."

"This tea shop thing—I could use a regular customer, and if you steal from her…" He didn't finish the sentence.

"I'm not going to steal from her," Kel said flatly.

"*You* aren't. What about Ezak?"

"Don't know. I haven't seen him."

"Is he angry with you about something?"

"Don't know."

Vezalis stared at him for a moment, then said, "Kelder, I know you don't like to talk if you don't need to, because your mouth got you in trouble when you were a kid, but please, tell me what's happening. Ezak is my only family, and if you two are going to do something stupid, I want to know about it."

Kel stared back, then looked at Dorna, who was waiting patiently. Then he turned back to Vezalis and said, "We went out to her village to try to steal her husband's magic, because you told Ezak about this dead sorcerer, only she figured out why we were there. She's *much* smarter than Ezak. She figured it out right away. But she needed some help moving stuff, so she pretended she hadn't, and we helped her while Ezak looked for a chance to steal all the magic. Except when he tried to steal it, he set off something with a name I can't pronounce that went and fixed up an old Northern thing that cut off part of Ezak's ear. I helped Dorna stop the Northern thing and get her magic back, and while we were doing that Ezak stole some of her other sorcery, but she had a magic tracker, so she came to Ethshar and found him and took it all back and said she'd kill him if he ever bothered her again. But *I* didn't steal anything from her, and I helped her, so she hired me to help with her tea shop, and I haven't seen Ezak since we took back her bag of magic."

"I saw the ear," Vezalis said. "He said it was cut off by a magic sword."

"Sort of," Kel said. The Northern sorcery had not been a sword, but he didn't have a better word for it.

"So you two—you argued? When you helped the sorcerer's widow get back her things?"

Kel shook his head. "Didn't argue. I went with Dorna."

"But you and Ezak—he's the closest thing to a family you have."

"He protected me," Kel agreed, nodding. "He took care of me. But he got me in trouble, too. A lot." He suddenly felt his eyes stinging, though he didn't know why. "I miss him, but I'm tired of being in trouble. I don't want to be a thief any more. I want to be Dorna's assistant. I wasn't a very good thief, but I think I can be a good assistant." He wiped a tear from his cheek; he was unsure how it had gotten there. "Tell Ezak I miss him, but as long as Dorna pays me, I'm not coming back to Smallgate."

Vezalis considered him for several seconds, then held out a hand. "I'll tell him," he said. "Good luck, Kelder."

Kel did not understand why Vezalis was using his full name, but he shook the offered hand, then turned and hurried to catch up with Dorna.

They walked several blocks up Archer Street in silence, but then Dorna said, "I wonder why he didn't invite us in?"

"He never invites *anyone* in," Kel said. "Not like that."

"Why not?"

"Watchdogs, partly," Kel said. "Not very well trained."

"Watchdogs?"

Kel nodded. "Three of them. Azrad, Anaran, and Gor."

Dorna smothered a laugh upon hearing that Vezalis had named his dogs for the founding overlords of the three Ethshars. "What do you mean, not well-trained?"

"They attack anyone except me, Ezak, Vezalis, and his two girlfriends," Kel explained. "Even if Vezalis is with them. If he had been home he would have locked them in the back room, but where he was outside with us..."

"...it would have been awkward," Dorna finished for him. "I see."

Kel knew he probably shouldn't say any more, but Vezalis had loosened his tongue, and he was not quite ready to tighten it again. "There's the merchandise, too," he said.

"What merchandise?"

"*All* his merchandise. Doesn't have a warehouse anymore. Keeps everything in his house. That's why he needs so many dogs."

Dorna glanced back at the house. "He keeps everything in *there*?"

Kel nodded. "He *used* to have a warehouse, long ago. But he took all his money and bought a ship and it sank, so he didn't have any money when there was a fire at the warehouse, so he couldn't rebuild it, and…well, now he keeps everything in his house and does all his traveling on land, with his cart, the way he came to your village."

"That explains a lot," Dorna said.

"He was traveling when his sister died—Ezak's mother. They'd had a fight when she took up whoring, so they hadn't spoken in years. He hadn't even known she had a baby. By the time he got back and heard from the magistrate that she was dead and that he had a nephew, Ezak was living in an alley. He'd been turned away from his uncle's house when he first went there. Vezalis found Ezak, but they didn't get along very well. Later he got Ezak an apprenticeship, even though no one was sure whether he was really only twelve, but it didn't work out, and Vezalis blamed Ezak for messing it up, and Ezak blamed Vezalis for trying to make him do something he didn't want to, and they haven't had much to do with each other since then. We stayed in his attic sometimes, because he didn't trust us around his merchandise in the other rooms, but Ezak never liked it."

"I can understand that," Dorna said quietly. "You and Ezak and Vezalis have had more than your share of misfortune, haven't you?"

Kel turned up an empty palm.

"Well, you don't need to live in alleys or cellars or attics anymore," she said.

Kel smiled happily at that.

FOURTEEN

Dorna's Tea Shop had been open for business for a little over a month, and the worst of the summer's heat had settled over the city like a thick blanket, when Ezak finally came to see the place. It was the middle of a cloudless, scorching afternoon. The big double door in the corner, facing out onto the intersection of Harbor and Aristocrat, was standing wide, and the windows on either side were open as well, to catch whatever breeze might reach so far into the city. Kel was sitting behind the counter on a stool in the back corner, idly waving a paper fan at himself as he gazed out at the dusty streets.

There were no customers; it was too warm to drink hot tea, and Kel did not yet know how to operate Dorna's sorcerous cooling device, so he could not offer the chilled version that was becoming popular. Dorna herself was down at the docks in Seagate with Vezalis, overseeing the arrival of the latest shipment from Londa, and Irien was over in the Merchants' Quarter, inspecting Ozya the Cabinetmaker's latest handiwork, so Kel had the place to himself.

Ezak seemed to appear out of nowhere in the doorway, but Kel was not impressed; he knew that trick himself. Ezak had taught him when they were both just boys. "*Hai*!" he called, with a wave of his fan. "Come in out of the sun!"

Ezak sauntered in, looking around appraisingly at the elegant little tables, the stylish silk-upholstered chairs, the shelves of cups and teapots and canisters—and the bare spaces that had once again sent Irien to Ozya's shop; they had not yet finished furnishing the place.

"Very fancy," Ezak said. "Uncle Vezalis said I could find you here."

"I'm glad to see you," Kel said. "How are you?" He was gradually learning to talk more freely, now that he had no secrets to hide and needed to please customers. It was hard to make out details with the sun silhouetting Ezak against the door, but Kel could see that Ezak was wearing an unfamiliar tunic, one that fit better than most. His boots were still reinforced with rags, though, and the fact that he was wearing boots at all in this heat meant he had no sandals. The top of his ear was still missing, but the wound had healed, and the missing hair had mostly grown back.

"I'm doing just fine," Ezak said. "See this?" He plucked at the front of his tunic. "Look at that embroidery!"

Kel, who knew the tunic had almost certainly been snatched off a clothesline somewhere, was no more impressed by this than by the appearing-around-the-corner trick. "It's nice," he said. He did not point out his own new tunic, which was plain white cotton, but had been acquired legally.

"We haven't seen you in Smallgate lately," Ezak said. "Nor in Grandgate Market."

"I've been busy," Kel said. "I live here in Nightside now. My room's upstairs."

"She's keeping you prisoner?"

Kel blinked in surprise. "No," he said.

"Then why are you still here?"

"I *like* it here!"

Ezak snorted. He looked around appraisingly, then he came closer and leaned across the polished wooden counter. "Some of this stuff looks expensive."

"Some of it was," Kel agreed.

"The door's wide open, and the nearest guard's at least three blocks away."

Kel simply stared at him. He realized he shouldn't be surprised that Ezak's immediate reaction was to think about robbing the place, but somehow he *was* surprised. Maybe he really had stopped thinking like a thief.

"Does she still have any of her husband's magic?"

Kel carefully did not look at the cooling talisman under the counter not three feet from his knee. "Yes," he said. "But it's all safely locked away."

Ezak nodded, and looked around the shop again, completely failing to see what was going through Kel's mind.

Kel, for his part, was realizing that he had just lied to Ezak, and Ezak had accepted it immediately. He had never been able to fool Ezak before.

"So if you took one of those fancy teapots and came home with me, could she track you?" Ezak asked.

"Probably," Kel said. He suppressed a smile at the idea of stealing a teapot when the cash box was right there under the counter, and held at least ten rounds in copper and a few bits in silver—not to mention that there was the cooling talisman, and the various sorcerous devices in the back room, that he could take.

For that matter, the savings he had tucked away under the floorboards of his room upstairs might be more than the teapot was worth, and were almost certainly more than they could get for it from a fence.

Now, if the animated teapot Dorna had ordered had been there, *that* might have been worth stealing, but it wasn't due to be delivered for another twelvenight.

"That explains why you're here alone, I guess," Ezak said. "She knows you don't dare steal anything."

"I guess," Kel said. He saw no point in trying to explain to Ezak that it wasn't fear that restrained him.

Ezak stepped closer and leaned on the counter, looking down at Kel. "So when are you coming home? Aren't you tired of this yet?"

Kel blinked up at him, and thought for a moment before replying honestly, "No."

"Oh, come on, Kel! She has you running stupid little errands and sitting here all day and saying please and thank you and bowing to all these rich bastards who come in here paying ridiculous prices for a bunch of boiled leaves. How can you stand it?"

"I *like* it," Kel said. "I like sleeping in a good bed, and eating three meals a day, and talking to people who aren't afraid I'm going to steal their purses. I like not having to run and hide, and not worrying whether I'm going to be dragged in front of the magistrates and sentenced to another flogging."

"But you're *trapped* here!"

"I can leave any time I want, Ezak. I just don't want to."

"How can you not *want* to?"

"I'm comfortable here."

"But people are telling you what to do all the time!"

Kel turned up a palm. "I'm used to that, Ezak. It's just that it always used to be *you* telling me what to do."

"I did not! I'm your friend! I always took care of you, didn't I?"

"Yes, you did," Kel agreed. "But I'm a grown man now. I can take care of myself."

Ezak stared at him. "You didn't think so a couple of months ago."

"I know," Kel said. "I was scared."

"Well, yes! It's a big nasty world, and you're a small fellow. You need someone to protect you."

Kel shook his head. "No, I don't," he said.

"Of course you do," Ezak said bitterly. "You just think the sorcerer's widow can do it better than I can now."

"No," Kel said. "She doesn't take care of me; she showed me that I could take care of myself."

"*I* took care of you!"

"You did," Kel agreed again. "But I don't want you to anymore. I do it better myself."

"Better? You call this *better*?" He waved at the shop.

"Yes."

"It's a trap! A prison! You'll need to work your whole life, until you fall over dead!"

"At least I won't starve, or get a knife in the back," Kel replied.

"You'll certainly never get rich!"

"I didn't get rich with you, either."

"Not *yet*, but one of these days I'll find a way, and I'll do it without taking orders from anyone."

Kel looked at him. "You never wanted to be a potter, did you?"

"What? Of course not! My uncle *made* me take that apprenticeship."

"You got kicked out on purpose."

"Yes, of course!"

"You didn't really try to join the guard that time, did you?"

"No, I just told Uncle Vezalis that."

"*I* tried, when I was about sixteen. I was too short."

"I...you did?" Ezak stepped back from the counter.

Kel nodded. "I don't want to be a thief, Ezak. I *never* wanted to be a thief."

"You didn't?"

"No."

Ezak stared at him. "Never?"

"Never."

Obviously shaken, Ezak said, "I don't believe you!"

Kel turned up both palms.

For a moment Ezak simply stared. Then he stepped forward and leaned on the counter again. "She has you under a *spell*, doesn't she?" he asked in a hoarse whisper.

"No," Kel said, amused.

"But you might not *know*," Ezak insisted. "She could have ensorcelled you without you knowing it."

Kel shook his head. "I don't think so." He thought, but did not say, that if he had been under anyone's spell, it was Ezak's—his words and attention had been as effective as magic in keeping Kel's loyalty. But the spell was broken now. All it had really taken was some time away from him, in the company of honest people. That, and watching how Dorna had set about building a new life when her husband's death destroyed her old one.

"Well, *I* think so," Ezak said. "I'm going to find a way to get you out of here, and then you'll help me steal Nabal's talismans, and we'll go to Ethshar of the Spices, or Ethshar of the Rocks, and use them to get rich. She knows too much about our places here."

Kel looked sadly up at Ezak. "We might be able to find you a job," he said. "Maybe you could still join the guard after all."

"I'm not taking anyone's orders! If you weren't enchanted, you'd know that!"

"I'm not enchanted. I grew up."

"Well…well, *stop* it!" To Kel's astonishment, he saw tears in Ezak's eyes. "You can't grow up! You're younger than me!"

"I'm…I'm twenty, I think. About that. That's grown up."

"It doesn't have to be!"

"I *want* to be," Kel said quietly. "I'm sorry, Ezak."

"You can rot, Blabbermouth!" Ezak said. He straightened up and spat at Kel. "If you never wanted to be a thief, why didn't you *tell* me?"

"I was scared."

"Of me?"

"Of everything. Including you."

Ezak looked around. "I should smash all this crockery. Then Dorna would throw you out and you'd have to come back to Smallgate."

"No, I wouldn't. I'd find someplace else. I'm not coming back."

Ezak glared at him.

"If you break anything, I'll call the guard," Kel added.

"You'd do that?"

Kel nodded.

"You'd do that to *me*?"

"Yes."

"You took a flogging for me last year!"

Kel nodded again.

"You aren't coming back? There's no way I can convince you?"

"No."

For a moment, the two men stared at each other. Then Kel said, "I'll miss you. I've missed you ever since you stole Dorna's bag."

"Well, you can go on missing me!" He turned to go.

"If you ever change your mind and want a job, I'll try to help," Kel called after him.

Ezak paused in the doorway. "If the spell ever breaks and you come to your senses, and you want to be free again, you know where to find me."

"I do," Kel agreed.

"Goodbye, Kel."

"Goodbye, Ezak."

Kel got to his feet and stood behind the counter, his hands on the smooth polished wood, and watched as Ezak marched across Harbor Street, and turned the corner onto Tapestry. Then he sighed, and returned to his stool.

That had been strange. All his life Ezak had been there, a tower of strength, a symbol of safety, watching over him. Ezak had been big and strong and smart, wise in the ways of the world, guarding him against all the menaces that surrounded them, teaching him what he needed to know.

But here and now, Ezak had looked like a spoiled child who had just had his favorite toy taken away. He had seemed silly and selfish, frightened and weak. It was sad. Kel knew he would never again look up to Ezak in the same way he had for so long. Even if Ezak were to suddenly turn into a respectable citizen, their relationship was changed forever.

But everything else had changed, as well. The city that had always seemed so hostile welcomed him now that he was working an honest job. He was well-fed and well-housed; he was trusted, even respected. He had lost his protector and best friend, but he had gained the world.

That was a trade worth making. If the sorcerer's widow really had enchanted him, he hoped the spell never broke.

THE END